Cat Tales
of
Clanton Creek

Iowa Farm Cats Tell Their Stories

By Bonne Doron

✳✳✳

Illustrations by Marc Brault

Copyright © 2017 Bonne Doron

All rights reserved.

No part of this publication may be reproduced, distributed, or transmitted in any form or by any means, including photocopying, recording, or other electronic or mechanical methods, without the prior written permission of the publisher, except in the case of brief quotations embodied in critical reviews and certain other noncommercial uses permitted by copyright law.

For written permission, requests and other queries, email the publisher at iafarmcats@gmail.com.

ISBN: 978-0-692-94701-2

To Roselea

This book would never have been possible without your knowledge, wisdom, encouragement, and, most of all, your friendship.

INTRODUCTION

Instructors at every level of education would agree that teaching is labor-intensive and, while rewarding in many ways, takes focus, patience, and creativity. So often, we find ourselves talking together in the break room about challenges of teaching, even among those in different disciplines.

As a professor of English, speech, and literature at college, I discussed my teaching challenges with a professor in the human services program, but we also talked about our lives outside of teaching. She often regaled me with stories of the cattle farm she and her husband owned in southern Iowa. Her favorite topic was the farm cats she interacted with while she and her husband worked chores. She animated her stories of their antics with passion, demonstrating a perceptive understanding of the cat community and their behavior. Often she described the individual cats in the two families with their unique personalities, habits, and characteristics, so they eventually seemed almost human to me.

When I met these amazing felines, I understood my friend's enthusiasm and love for her farm friends. I even adopted two cats, one which became a pet therapy cat. Angel learned to walk on a leash, proudly strutting the halls at the VA hospital while talking with everyone along the way. One WWII vet called, "Bring that cat here. She looks just like the mouser from my farm!" Angel was such an extraordinary cat that she became a character in the book.

One day I said, "You know. Someday, I should write down some of your information about your cats as fictional stories. You tell me about the cats and what they do, and I'll write a book about them ... and you." Having no idea what that would mean or if I was serious, we'd laugh. Until one day, I created the first story about Cream Puff, based on her memory of him. So this book was born.

Because I wanted the cats to be as relatable and interesting as possible to my readers without anthropomorphizing them, each character was based on an actual cat on the farm telling its own "real" story, in addition to the daily life of a cat community.

This book is collaboration. My co-professor and I worked side-by-side as she kept me from embarrassing myself with farm misinformation. I had a lot to learn about farm life. I had to learn the difference among steers, heifers, and cows, and all cats sometimes hunt.

Not only was she a patient teacher, but she proved herself adept at editing, evaluating illustrations, mapmaking, and researching. A woman of many talents! Most of all, she was a good friend, who encouraged me when I became discouraged with the challenging literary process, guiding me with her intuitive and creative solutions. My friend is Leah, the wife of Farmer Bob, who cares for the cats on their farm where Clanton Creek runs through the property and many of the stories.

I am often asked just who the intended audience might be. It is definitely not a true children's book as the vocabulary is advanced but is more appropriate for, at the earliest, an adolescent reader. That being said, I can imagine an adult reading the book to very young listeners with their Paws or Spunky at their sides. But it is mostly intended for any lover of animals who are family members. Finally, these stories apply to human communities as well as the cats because they reflect the human condition.

Enjoy!

ACKNOWLEDGMENTS

How does one thank all who were responsible for this book? First, many thanks go to Roselea Johnson, who never lost sight of the potential for this book. I owe her everything!

And to the many people who encouraged me to continue writing for many years, and those who didn't roll their eyes when I said I was still writing a book. They never showed a doubt that one day this would reach the library book shelves. Their confidence in my determination and efforts kept me going. Thanks, Glen, for your faith in me!

To my faithful editors, Sue Wickham and Andrew McFadyen-Ketchum. Sue worked each rough chapter with such dedication as if they were her own stories. Her instincts on literary components were absolutely to be trusted, and I appreciated her patience and sensitivity to my concerns while advising me. Andrew was an editor who worked every sentence with skill, cutting out unnecessary verbiage but making it easy to accept his advice for improving the book.

I thank also the beta-readers, those friends who read the book and made helpful suggestions: Michelle Mosman, Jean Rothfusz, Nancy Roath, Sandi Kirk, and Margaret Samuel. Special thanks to Christine Stoffa, a long time church buddy who for years asked how the book was coming along with genuine enthusiasm. She was the first reader who reacted as if she was actually witnessing their narratives. When she caught a mistake in a character's name, her reaction was "Oh dear, Puff the Protector got his old name back! Bet he is not happy." Thanks to Marykaye Madden for the gift of a book on self-publishing and her confidence in me. Finally, my gratitude to Anne Parker, the professional formatter and fine-tuner of the book. She had excellent creative ideas for improvements from the inside pages to the front and back covers. She was a joy to work with.

Thanks also to Marc Brault, an illustrator extraordinaire. I was impressed with his realistic drawings of animals and his faithful attention to background details, and, at the same time, his skill at illustrating their individual characters. Marc knew exactly what needed to be in each illustration.

Most of all, I thank my Creator who provided me with each one of you as well as with my education, job opportunities, teaching experiences, and expertise. So many times I almost put the manuscript on the shelf with discouragement or lack of confidence, but He just wouldn't have it. He orchestrated every step of the process. You are the source of it all!

CONTENTS

A Day in the Life of the Cat Community 1

The Stranger. 15

Puff: Protector of Kittens 21

Hunter Arrives 37

Bear 47

Furball's Death and Funeral 61

Ivan 69

FDR 81

Ghost Eyes 91

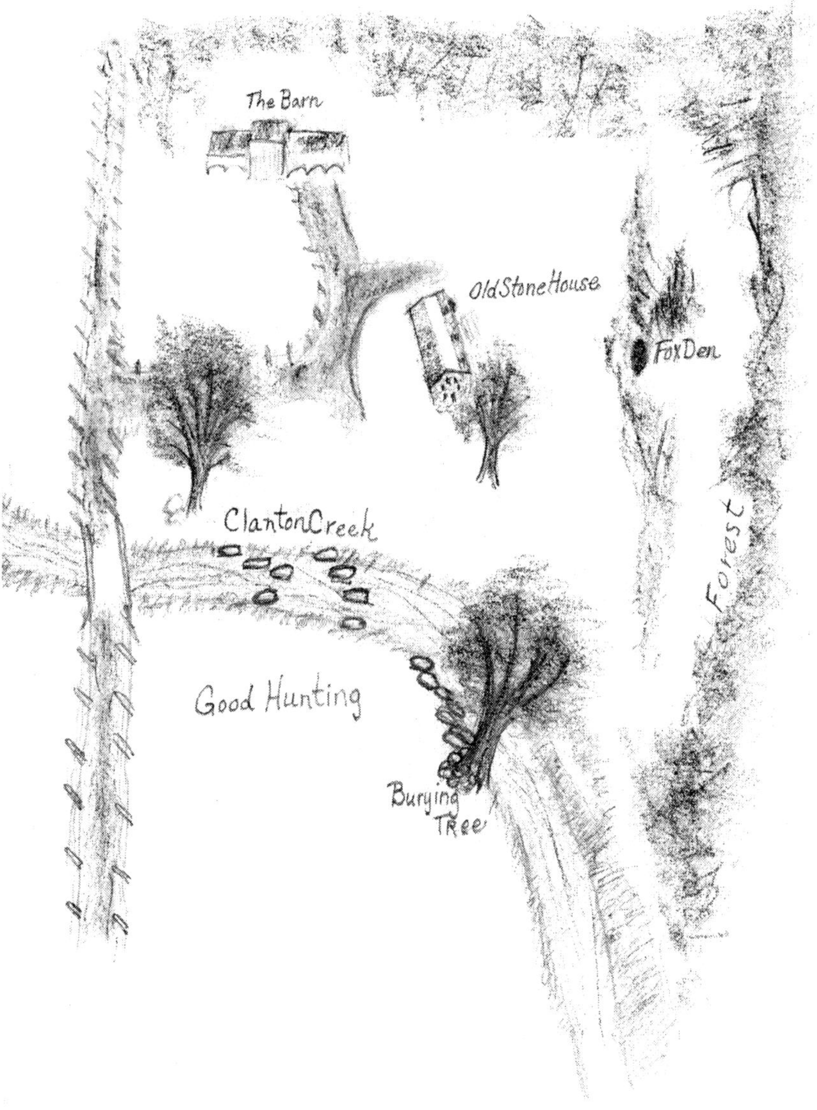

The Barn

Old Stone House

Fox Den

Clanton Creek

Forest

Good Hunting

Burying Tree

Descendants of Cinder

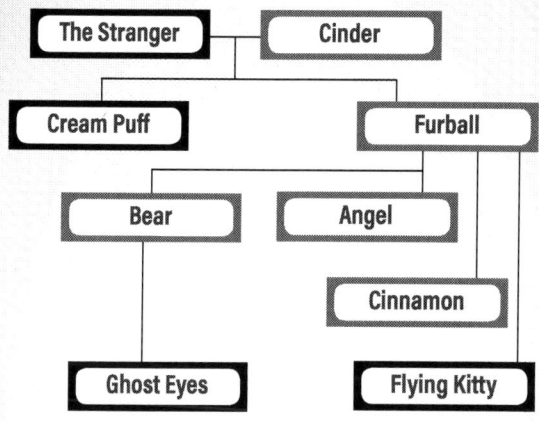

Descendants of Hunter

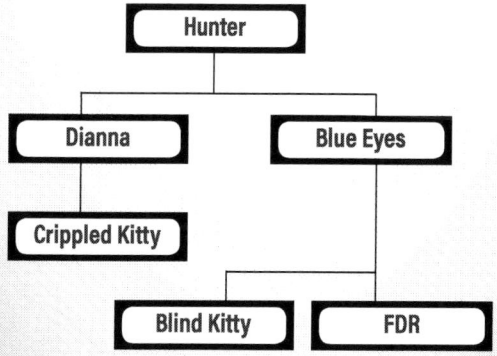

CAT TALES
of
Clanton Creek

CAT TALES OF CLANTON CREEK

CHAPTER 1

A Day in the Life of the Cat Community

GHOST EYES' CHARCOAL-GRAY FUR MAKES HIM APPEAR more like a ghost than flesh and blood. When he hunts in pale light of late afternoon in the woods behind Farmer Bob and Leah's cattle farm, one can never be sure if it's an animal or the spirit of one. His brooding, deep set eyes peering out beneath a shelf of striped eyebrows adds to his spooky, phantom appearance.

This afternoon, Ghost Eyes sits in a peaceful pose of recline. He yawns widely, his eyes lazy slits as he dozes in a warm stream of setting sun. These eyes reflect past generations of his long-haired clan.

Ghost Eyes is a throw-back of many generations of long-haired farm cats. Whereas Cinder and The Stranger were the first parents of that family, Ghost Eyes might be the last of his kind. His wide neck ruff, draping hair, tufted paws, feathery ears, and sweeping whiskers identify him as, most likely, a descendant of a Maine Coon line, originating with The Stranger, Cinder's choice of mate.

As if a sudden electric current hits, his back paw twitches. He snatches at it, chews vigorously, and then settles back down into his reverie. His front paws are neatly tucked under his muscular body. His tail settles down to a casual sweeping motion.

"How I love lazing around on these sunny afternoons. I'd rather do this than participate in the farm cat community like most members. I do interact within the community, of course, but mostly observe it from the surrounding hills. Of course, I love to breed with the farm's females and others as I wander the neighborhood. I can coexist in both my separate world and still participate in communities when I want.

"I love spending time with Leah, Farmer Bob's wife, above all else. When she calls me from the far fields for my evening meal, I come running to gobble from my own bowl in the stone house rather than eat at the community food bowl. Unlike most of the other males—but definitely in keeping with long-haired traits—I'm very much connected to people, especially Leah, the provider of my favorite brand of cat food and affectionate rubs. We enjoy long chatty conversations, discussing my day on the stone house steps after dinner or walking alongside her in the fields, advising her how to dig up those pesky thistles.

"But, you know," Ghost Eyes declares, "I still love the wild with its meals of slow birds and careless rabbits. I enjoy visiting with the females all over my territory, so I can be confident of kittens to carry on my genes. I could easily survive without humans. But I must have time with my Leah. She helps this cat community thrive with her daily meals, caring for the sick, providing funeral services, socializing the young kittens, and communicating with us as if we were equals. In general, she is our most favorite friend!" Ghost Eyes smiles with serene contentment as he scans the farm.

"No matter where I am, I try to keep within earshot of the farm, especially in late afternoon as the sunlight fades into the darkening sky. If I miss a day or more without talking with her, I make sure I'm ready to come running when she calls me for dinner." He shakes his fluffy neck ruff like a lazy lion and then again furiously bites his back paw, cursing the ticks embedded in his fur.

"Leah was there when my great, great, great grandmother Cinder first met The Stranger who gave us Furball, our most revered alpha. Leah thought the long-hairs were extinct after a vicious assault on the cats in the window well, so most of the later generations did not resemble the original, long-haired Stranger. But then I was born with my pensive personality and eyes she said resembled those of a ghost, eyes that gazed back into the past and forward into the future." He settles back into a resting pose with his front paws folded into each other in arcs of grey fur. His eyes slowly close.

"I know our community. Its characters and traditions are a blend of the wild and domestic. So we farm cats live by nature as well as by contact with humans. An odd but highly effective community.

"We operate like most societies. There are specified times for work, play, and socializing with other cats and species, including humans. Time for mating, birthing, and parenting. Time for survival. And time inevitability for death. Sometimes these events happen at random, depending on many factors. Weather. Time of year. The personalities of the individual cats. Our blood lines. The nature of the resident alpha or simply at the whim of nature itself.

"The reason I can be both a part of the community as well as independently is that feline families and communities work both individually and as a cooperative unit. The different members function in distinct roles and purposes in their families and collectively in the community as well. They establish clear hierarchy of ranking members within a matriarchal social structure.

"The most important role is that of the leader, usually known as the 'alpha.' The others in the group must show respectful deference to their alpha by posture, behavior, and even sounds. The alphas have first priority to eat, to select and breed with their preferred mates, and even to lead the pack in different activities.

For example, when Furball—an athletic, confident cat—was reigning alpha, in late winters she chose any male she wanted to mate with and became pregnant before any of the other females in the community. Like humans, status has its privileges.

"The alpha cats achieve this status with their physique, superior abilities, personality, age, length of time in the group, their family's status, and sometimes by challenging and, if possible, displacing the existing alpha. However, on Leah and Farmer Bob's farm, alphas descend only from our long-haired clan, never from the short-hairs. Only once, in fact, was the long-hair alpha ever seriously challenged by a short-hair. Although I tried to warn that cat, her challenge resulted in her banishment.

"Legend has it that Furball acted like an alpha should," Ghost Eyes said thoughtfully. "She had confidence. She was assertive, interacting with us with firmness, but always with her self-assured grin. Even her posture spoke of her status: she walked with head held high and feet prancing. She was our proud leader!

"Cat communities have one alpha at a time, sometimes for many generations and sometimes for a few weeks. Or the leadership can simply be a matter of chance. When available alphas cannot serve due to illness, aging, or death, other cats have the opportunity to take over that position. One cannot predict the length of an alpha's time in power, but the community always has one.

"In many situations, the members cooperate collectively. When the community is threatened, for example, they will work together to confront the intruder and get the kittens to safety. I was able to escape one of the greatest threats we ever had, a truly evil cat. Even today, I admonish the young to obey with 'Remember the evil one!'"

"The community's first priority is hunting for food. This job includes all cats, except for the kittens and the infirm. Although the humans feed us twice a day, farm cats need more calories to function. Just keeping warm in subzero temperatures necessitates much more sustenance than we get from Leah and Farmer Bob. We know this intuitively for survival. We can't simply depend on humans to provide all of our food. Plus, we felines love the fun of the hunt itself. Females do most of the hunting although with the help of us males. I usually hunt in the afternoons in far fields or woods, taking advantage of the warming sun. Being nocturnal, we cats can hunt at night as well because we see even the smallest creature in the dark as though we are wearing night vision goggles.

"As beautiful and prominent as the long-hairs are, Hunter, Dianna, and the other members of the short-haired clan are the hunting professionals. Hunter, the first of the short-hairs, is a calico with hues of black, orange, and white. Her daughter, Dianna wears a much darker background, sharing similar coloring with her mother. Their bodies are built for hunting: they are wiry with thin but powerful leg bones and toned muscles, and their coloring camouflages their movements. These hunters can outjump, outrun, and almost out-hear their prey, daily bringing in the tastiest morsels.

"Just watch Hunter over there. She can jump effortlessly as high as a human! Hunter is waiting patiently under a burning bulb above the entrance to the stone house, carefully monitoring the insects diving around and knocking against it, creating a rhythmic song that mesmerizes her. Then, without so much as a tense muscle or an apparent crouched position, she rises up as if on wings and snatches a moth or June bug in mid flight in a blur of paws and tails before twisting in the air to simply float back to the ground, landing squarely on her feet. She munches on her catch and looks up nonchalantly as she prepares for another successful leap. You can see why we call them 'high leapers,'" explains Ghost Eyes with deep respect. "Believe me, we long-hairs couldn't compete with Hunter and her daughters!"

"The shorthairs' camouflage makes them particularly exquisite hunters at dusk and even during a full moon. Dianna's variegated colors enable her to literally disappear, a magician's optical illusion. The black patches blend into the night's darkness, so that she can move almost unnoticed, even in an exposed area. When the moon's dappled shadows fall on her yellow shoulder patches, you can't see her silhouette. She looks just like another part of the scenery. If I can't see her, I'll bet she is almost invisible and undetectable by prey and enemy alike. Once, I thought I saw Dianna hunting at night but couldn't be sure because her coloring looks as if she were spattered with different colored paint. Thus, if hunting is required, Hunter and Dianna dominate with their lissome bodies, jumping expertise, and camouflage.

"Since I'm kind of lazy, my favorite way to get a fine meal is by waiting under the feed bunks where cattle eat their shelled corn. Cattle are notoriously sloppy, moving their heads to-and-fro as they eat, spilling mouthfuls of grain on the ground. When hungry mice or rats come to clean up the grain, we cats lurk to 'clean' them up. Wild turkeys also feed at this dinner table, but cats dare not challenge such large birds.

"Once, a wary mouse was helping itself to a meal, unaware that I was spying from behind the feed trough. Silently, I dropped to a crouch and crept up as closely as I could without detection. Then, like a streak of summer lightning, I sprang! It must have detected my presence in the nick of time for it didn't even turn around before it darted away mid-chew. I hated to be so close, yet it slipped away," added Ghost Eyes as he slowly shook his head from side to side in memory of his frustration.

"So many feeding opportunities exist for the feline hunters, even if it is provided by other hunters. When hunting cats return with their booty, they often share their food with older or injured cats who can't feed themselves. We are proud of our giving from our abundance to those who can't provide for themselves.

"As important as hunting is, play is almost equally important to the community's welfare. Although play doesn't keep the community fed, sport for fun's sake is required for our physical, emotional, and social well being. It provides social interaction, relationships and bonding. Play also hones our physical skills and helps us relax after a stressful day.

"I remember those fun afternoons in the barn 'Riding the Rafters.' The participating cats are called 'Crossbeam Runners' or 'Rafter Runners.' The sport originated with Furball, her daughter Angel, and the other athletic long-hairs, stocky and built low to the ground with thick muscular legs. They gathered where the hay was stored in the barn which supported diagonal boards connected to high, horizontal rafters. The cats gathered at the base of one of these slanted planks and, with Furball in the lead, scrambled up the boards to the high woven rafters, scurrying all over the crossbeams, more like birds than land-bound creatures. They raced without hesitation, rarely missing a step or having to balance, sprinting and loping and dodging each other in a mock battle of bravery. And while this was all in good fun, 'Riding the Rafters' could profit them if they were able to catch a pigeon or sparrow that happened to be roosting on one of the rafters. One must be a tightrope artist to catch a bird on these balance beams, but these 'Rafter Runners' were surprisingly successful. We could hear them laughing and shouting challenges to each other as they dashed, perfectly balanced, along the rafters. Some of us less agile cats, like me and Bear, Angel's heavy, raven-colored sister, preferred to remain on the barn floor, cheering the aerial family to greater feats. My ancestors," adds Ghost Eyes, his chest puffing with pride, "spent hours playing this game.

"Play can involve the humans too! When Leah or Farmer Bob become part of the fun, these times allow them to bond with us and to appreciate our unique personalities. Bob is usually very busy and focused on raising cattle, demanding work such as calving, inoculating, and feeding as well as planting crops and making hay for the cattle. But when he has a moment of free time, he can be found playing too.

"I wish you could see Flying Kitty, a male who looked like a longer version of Furball. Flying Kitty would plant his paws on Farmer Bob's legs, look up, and loudly beg for a flight! Farmer Bob cradled the cat in the curve of his arm and carried him to the flat yard. There, he hoisted the cat high into the air. But not to worry! He never flung Flying Kitty too far, and cats always land firmly on their feet," Ghost Eyes added with pride, "And with practice, Farmer Bob launched Flying Kitty farther and farther until it looked as if he was flying! But the real fun was when, after landing in a graceful pose, that cat would race back and beg for another trip. Flying Kitty repeated this for as long as Farmer Bob was willing to play. In fact, he often sought out the farmer doing his chores for more aviation lessons. I was never brave enough to try flying," Ghost Eyes smiled at the thought. "Only Flying Kitty was courageous and trusting enough to 'fly'.

"Sometimes, play is individualized. Furball always told us that one of her best friends was a gentle calf called Blackie. Leah put her on Blackie's shoulders when the calf was only a yearling, 'just for fun,' she told Farmer Bob standing nearby with worry stitched across his brow. At first, Furball rode Blackie with her claws gripped tightly to Blackie's thick coat, but with time, she frequently asked Leah to put her up on her friend and rode the huge heifer with confidence, relaxed with her typical smile spread wide across her face. Furball and Blackie became close friends. Furball was often seen leaping over the mounds of black mud in the barn yard to greet Blackie and touch noses. She would slurp at her feline friend with her long, snakelike tongue, almost knocking Furball over with its sheer strength. Cross-species friendships are not as rare as humans think, even in the wild itself.

"One daily activity that involves all generations and ages is greeting Farmer Bob and Leah by jumping on their truck or car when they arrive at the farm. The couple lives in the city, not on the farm, but daily drives to the farm. We start to gather, eager with anticipation, when we hear the grinding sound of the truck's gears or the purr of the car's engine as they make their way up the steep driveway. When the humans finally shut off the motor, the 'Greeters' jump on the hood, ready for the fun.

"Kittens can participate as soon as they grow big enough to maneuver onto the hood. It is considered a rite of passage when a kitten becomes large and strong enough to jump on the hood all on its own. Furball's brother, Cream Puff, who loves to interact with kittens, encourages them to climb up as he calls to them with an entreating meow from the hood. For the pure enjoyment of jumping on top of the roof and sliding down the windshield and chasing the driver's finger through the windshield, 'Greeters' scurry all over the vehicle with pure delight.

"Then it's time for 'Follow the Leader.'" Ghost Eyes' paws twitches ever so slightly as he reminisces. "We run all over the dusty surface of the vehicle, leaving paw prints and, on other days, we leave muddy slide marks behind. Then, we line up in various positions of sitting or stretching or lying where the hood meets the windshield, grooming ourselves from tip to stern. Finally, once we are satisfied that we are clean, we settle down with slit eyes to soak up the sun's beams and the warmth radiating from the metal hood. What a show for the humans inside the vehicle! But as soon as a door opens, we all stop what we are doing, race to the house and begin loudly begging for food.

"Many of the chatty long-hairs love to accompany the humans on their chores around the farm. Whether Farmer Bob is repairing machinery or Leah is digging thistles far in a distant field, Furball, her daughters, sons, or grandchildren often follow them single-file, tails pointed straight up like so many soldiers carrying bayoneted rifles. It is serious business watching the humans' progress and making very vocal recommendations as the humans perform their daily tasks. These trips simply keep the humans company. So when Leah calls, 'Come, kitties! Come kitties! Time to dig thistle,' all available cats come running as fast as they do when she calls them for dinner and discuss the tasks to be accomplished all the way from the house to the field. Some of us like to hitch a ride to the fields on her shoulder or hip, looking forward to the day's work.

"Leah looks like the Pied Piper followed by such a company of cats. Once she arrives at the slope of the pasture, I always wait in the shade of the ravine while she digs up thistles. If she gets too far away, I call 'her back' across the hill, reminding her I'm still waiting. I am," Ghost Eyes added, "particularly adept at communicating in general, but especially while Leah works. In fact, it is my favorite way of connecting with this human. Advising and communicating are serious business for us cats.

"Some of the activities seem to do with normal functions of the cat community but are also to guarantee our survival, especially of the dominant long-haired clan. When Furball shared her kitten's nest with her daughters and sisters, all kittens were nursed by which-ever mother was nearest. This sharing is important not only for her kittens' survival, but also giving Furball's kittens the longest nursing period, assuring they would become the biggest and most mature kittens on the farm. Furball knew the fittest had to be specially provided for to insure that the alpha position remained within her family. Protecting the health of her kittens took place when Furball transferred a sickly kitten to the Hunter's nest until it recovered. She kept order and retained dominance even at the mealtime bowl. I learned to back off and let kittens eat first when she placed her paw firmly on my forehead.

"My most vivid childhood memory was when our mothers took us kittens "camping," as Leah calls it, in the distant fields. This experience is an unusual, yet necessary aspect of every kitten's survival training. It happens shortly after kittens are ready to be weaned and are able to eat whole food.

"We weren't expecting anything unusual when the mothers called us kittens to go out hunting. We trailed after our mothers, getting distracted by catching a grasshopper or investigating an interesting crevice in an oak tree when suddenly we discovered we were alone. The mothers went back to the stone house and waited for their kittens to return. By sticking together and foraging for small rodents and chasing plenty of grasshoppers, we kittens didn't go hungry. But, for the first time in our lives, we didn't have any warm milk before bedtime.

"That first night of camping was very scary, but we all kept together by huddling closely to each other for warmth and protection. If anyone heard a crack or a rustle in the ground cover, we all clawed up a nearby tree as fast as we could. I was too scared to sleep that night. We knew to stick together, not leaving any stragglers who could become a meal for a fox or a raccoon. The next morning, we decided we would have to figure out how to find our way home. Finally, we began seeing familiar sights and quickly found the stone house.

"When we saw our mothers, we ran toward them with much loud complaining, relief, and vigorous rubbing up against them. They greeted us, licking us to clean and straighten our fur, but they didn't give us any warm milk for supper. After this rite of passage, I knew I had the hunting and survival skills to make it on my own. You know," added Ghost Eyes, "I suspect that maybe many of the mothers followed us from a distance or checked up on us at night, not allowing their kittens to hear or see them, and leaving when we woke, ready to find our way home. I'll bet a mother was never ever too far away, always within ear-shot of us little campers.

"Despite all these efforts to ensure the community's survival, inevitably, death comes to us all. In fact, the lifespan of a farm cat is brief compared to our domesticated counterparts. We rarely reach old age, living only a few seasons of adulthood. There are too many natural predators—with domesticated dogs near the top of the list. And then there's weather, and untimely births—such as stubble cats born after oats have been cut, too near winter—and many other common causes of our demise. Even kind and careful humans can cause our death in a rare accident.

"Just as is the case with humans, one of the most solemn times in farm cats' lives is when they experience a fellow cat's death, especially if it is an alpha. A good alpha never to be duplicated," explains Ghost Eyes, "but we cats understand that leaving this existence is part of life. We accept death as much as we embrace life. We know the community survives and continues to operate even after a great loss of our leader.

"So the cat community remains ordered even as it endures being taken over by a new alpha as if tagged by the ghost of the previous leader of our community. I, Ghost Eyes, the last remnant of the long-hairs, embody my family's friendliness and stunning physical characteristics. In my reflective eyes, I preserve the memory of the long-hairs and the farm cat community, an offering of hope for my cat community's future.

"Oh, gotta run! Leah is calling me for supper. There are many more adventures about some of the more colorful members of the cat community that you'll find entertaining. Talk with you later!"

A Day in the Life of the Cat Community

CHAPTER 2

The Stranger

"HEY! WHAT WAS THAT?" CINDER CRIED. "There, at the east end of the shed? It looks a little like one of those pesky raccoons, but it can't be! The stripes and color seem right, but it moves all wrong!" Cinder tried to readjust her focus, straining forward, each muscle taut with attention. Because of the low light of dusk, she couldn't be sure of what she saw move in the shadows.

She inched forward, one paw lightly touching the ground like the first tentative step of a slow dance. She knew she was safe because her deep black coloring camouflaged her presence. On a moonless night like tonight, Cinder could move wherever she wished without being detected.

"Could it be one of us?" she asked herself. "The only cat nearly that big is Bob Cat. But this animal has a long, bushy tail—like some kind of mysterious monster. If my eyes aren't deceiving me, I'd swear that's the biggest raccoon I've ever seen."

The muscles beneath Cinder's ebony coat twitched with anxiety. As if in slow motion, she started to turn around. Farm cats usually don't stop to question when their senses warn of something unidentifiable or possibly dangerous; instinctively, they run. Fast! On the other hand, felines are naturally curious; her curiosity got the better of her this time. She stayed crouched in her flight stance—just in case— keeping the front wheels of Farmer

Bob's truck between her and this mysterious stranger. That rusty truck was a source of warmth in the winter and—in situations like these—of concealing protection.

"Whatever it is?" Cinder whispered to herself, "It has to be almost the length of Farmer Bob's wagon. And will you just look at those sweeping whiskers! It must be really heavy too—probably more than a bag of cattle feed! But what is it?"

Again Cinder stepped tentatively forward, ready to streak away or crawl into the belly of the truck if the strange beast charged in her direction. First one paw, then the other, she hesitated and then reach forward and stopped to focus and then slowly reached again with the opposite paw. Holding her breath, she kept her weight carefully balanced over her hips, so she could instantly rotate to escape.

"How can you tell what it is with all that massive hair?" she asked herself. "Shadowy gray with bold stripes. The size of a stupid dog. Huh? This can't be good..." She was just about to head up into the safety of the barn rafters, but she just couldn't. Again she stood frozen in place, almost against her will.

She waited for an answer. Her nerves taut and her legs starting to quiver. Still, she waited for the answer. And she waited. But no answer came.

"Should I run?" Cinder questioned, torn between fascination and fear of the unknown.

"But it's so odd looking!" Though drawn to the strange creature, she still had the presence of mind to obey her survival instincts, for which caution was always the rule. She knew she was alone; no one was even in ear-shot to help if something went wrong. But still—she had to know.

Sensing it was being observed, the nimble animal picked up speed and trotted alongside the shed. Leaping like an athlete over the farm equipment as deer leap fences surrounding a corn field, it moved quickly and with purpose, nothing like an animal in fear. As it loped, it stretched the full length of its neck and sniffed the air and everything else in its path.

"What is he?" Cinder wondered. Whatever species it was, its huge, furry legs, rugged paws, sturdy frame and muscular build all indicated it was definitely a "he." Trying to decide to move, she could only remain planted like a statue in a garden as she watched the mammoth beast move gracefully over the tops of the long line of barrels stacked against the shed's north wall. She had to get a closer look; she couldn't panic and retreat without knowing what this stranger was. He hurried a few steps—then froze, scanning the surrounding area before moving quickly forward—only to hesitate again. Cinder ducked her head and crouched to avoid being detected when he looked in her direction. The animal was distracted by sudden snatches of farm scents, compelling him to reach his full length to get a deep inhale of the smell. She could see the grimace of his open mouth after an inhale. Finally, the animal exited the shed and disappeared around the back.

At that moment, Cinder caught a whiff of something familiar in the breeze. Instantly, she recognized his graceful, continuous movement, every part of its body in perfect sync. A ringed snake flowing smoothly as it slipped through the grass.

"It's a CAT!" Cinder whispered a little too loudly. Wrinkling her nose, she sniffed the air to confirm her conclusion.

"Must be! I'd know that movement anywhere—now! But I've never seen any cat that big—ever! Not ever!"

"That fragrance is always in the wind," she reminded herself. Finally Cinder grinned ear-to-ear, accentuating her natural smile, her skin twitching in response to a familiar drive deep in her being.

"And this stranger is so fine!" she crooned in a soft meow. "Such magnificence and beauty and strength all rolled into one. Oh my!"

Cinder relaxed her tense legs, dipped into a crouch and sprinted out towards the back of the barn.

That was the beginning. Nine weeks later, Furball and Cream Puff arrived at the farm.

The Stranger

CHAPTER 3

Puff: Protector of the Kittens

THE PALE SUN COLORED THE BARN A FADED GRAY. Slanted light filtered down through the tree line in the west where strips of deep purple and fuchsia painted a vibrant canvas across the spring sky.

Farmer Bob and Leah had just rumbled away for the day in the truck. As soon as its dust plume evaporated, Cinder sounded her alarm, a sharp yowl so loud that every member of the cat community would hear her, even those wandering far off on late afternoon hunts. Knowing Cinder's call was no ordinary summons, every member of the community hurried to the barn and settled in a semicircle around her.

"We have a problem, my feline families," Cinder announced. Wide-eyed, the cats nervously looked at each other because of the urgency in her voice. Cinder only called them "felines" when she meant business. Their ears pricked up; they focused in on her every move. Not a hair trembled! Nor a muscle twitched! As alpha, Cinder remained alert to all threats to the cat community. It was her duty to spot any potential dangers and then warn the others.

"Either we protect our litters of kitten . . . !" Pausing for import, Cinder scanned each face in turn. "Or else!" Not one of them moved. No one dared even to glance at the stunning sunset.

"Or else what?" questioned a black-and-white tuxedo teen. Apparently, she was unaware of feline protocol: when summoned by the alpha, every cat was to remain stone still and silent.

"Or else we do not survive," Cinder replied in an emotionless voice that sent chills through the entire assembly. The teen immediately focused on her, chastised by Cinder's tone.

"As we all know, we have lost almost all our litters the past few months. As each of the sisters gives birth, within just a few weeks, we find every kitten dead...-or missing. At this rate, we will lose generations. And we cannot replace them!" The adults' heads bowed in memory of fallen members of the community. A huge yellow tabby shook his head from side to side in grief.

"What is killing them?" Furball, Cinder's eldest, cried out in alarm. Furball was learning how to lead as the heir to Cinder's alpha status. She had the most to lose in the crisis.

"Yeah!" the others meowed in unison.

"It could be anything or anyone" Cinder offered. "Maybe a predator like a coyote or even those pesky raccoons no matter how slow and bulky they are. Even we adults steer clear of raccoons when they raid our food. Or during the breeding season, it could be a male from the outside of the farm. Even our resident males sometimes take the kittens of their competition, so they can sire their own offspring." Several of the larger males shifted in their stiff postures, uncomfortable talking about their rivals. Even in the most closely-knit cat communities, toms—male cats—rival all other males for dominance. One solid black short-hair quietly backed out of the group and melted into the shadows of dusk.

Wanting to but nervous about contributing, Cream Puff stepped forward hesitantly. He usually left the discussions and decisions to his mother and sister, but now he wanted to participate.

"But we cannot watch the new litters all the time like we should. It's already our responsibility to rid the farm of mice and rats eating Farmer Bob's feed. We have to hone our survival skills when we hunt for food; it's not just food. If one of us stays back to guard the kittens, then the whole community could be in danger. We all must hunt!" Lowering his eyes, he returned to his place in the group.

Cream Puff ever-so-slightly relaxed from his tense state of alert. The rusty streaks of deep orange ribbing in his long, flowing fur were highlighted by his coat's cream background. Cinder's first male kitten and brother to Furball, Cream Puff always tried to avoid confrontation, with anyone or anything. He just didn't have the spirit of combat in his being! He's been known to let a half-pint, saucy kitten push him away from the community food bowl—a serious no-no in the community rules. And oh how he was teased! Using his name against him, especially the males loved to taunt him in their loudest singsong every time they saw him, particularly when he refused to participate in their jousting and practice fighting.

"Puff has no stuff!" they heckled.

"Don't get too rough with Puff!" they yowled.

"Not mean, just cream!" they yelled in deafening meows.

Cream Puff knew they were right; he had no courage.

Sometimes Furball defended him with growls of anger at their bullying. But the second she moved out of earshot, they went right back to it. Now with their teasing chants still fresh in his ears, his sides caved in on him, forcing him to lie down.

Will I ever feel good about myself, especially with my stupid name? he thought. *I'm so sick and tired of being humiliated all the time! Maybe I should just leave the farm.*

"Quite honestly," he admitted one time to Furball while they were lazing in the warm sun, "I have no stomach for fighting all these males, just to win a mate. I'd rather not have anything to do with the girls around here if I have to constantly impress them." Furball had rubbed against his cheek with affection, but he knew she understood his true fears.

Now, Cream Puff was tolerated or simply ignored by everyone but immediate family. His mother often took him aside after a particularly bad day of teasing and licked his wounded pride with her rough tongue until he felt better. When she was done, his coat shined with a cascading, butterscotch hue across his sturdy frame. Then he looked like a true member of the long-hair breed. Along with his extraordinary length and muscular form, even the females would look his way and the males secretly would envy his majestic beauty. Still, most of the time, Mother Cinder or Furball had to rebuild his confidence after another siege of hurtful name-calling.

They often encouraged him. "Oh Puff, don't forget you're son of The Stranger and Cinder, our founder. Be proud! You are from the long-haired family. The finest of felines!"

At other times, they assured him that, "Someday you will show those bullies! There is courage inside you, Cream Puff, son of our founding parents." Then Furball would gently touch her nose to his and generously lick each of his ears. Grooming always helped his wounded spirit.

So when Cinder dismissed the meeting, another male nudged him.

"Hey, Puff," he called in front of the whole crowd, "how's about proving your stuff? You don't do much around here anyway, no flirting with the females or jousting with us. But the kittens like you! Why not volunteer to guard them? Or are you too…" the antagonist paused for effect, "scared?"

The other males cheered their agreement. The mocking male slapped him between his shoulder blades, knocking him. Cream Puff moved away, shamed yet again.

"All I'm good for is babysitting kittens!" he scornfully murmured to himself when he resettled near the shaded opening of the barn. But instead of the heavy disgrace he usually felt, something else woke inside him. "Ya know, that's not a half-bad idea!" he thought out loud.

What the males shouted was, indeed, true. He often found himself in the middle of groups of kittens, playing hide-and-seek with them, or letting them tumble and roll all over him in mock combat. They'd hiss their little threats and jump on him with all fours as he pretended to be frozen with fear. Or he would spar with them, shielding his own claws as they hung on his neck ruff and mouthed their defiance.

"They don't mean any harm," he once assured Furball. "They're just practicing for the big time. Maybe I can help them do that even if I can't do it myself."

Cinder had also noticed her son's effective training techniques when she discovered his mock fight with an adolescent, sable-colored runt who thought he had knocked his elder down.

"Atta boy, Panther! Well done!" Cream Puff yelled as he righted himself. "You almost got me then," he offered as he ruffled the youngster's head with an affectionate cuff.

Panther smiled up at Puff with pride.

"Someday you'll be a great dad!" Cinder predicted. "Your love for these tiny ones will undoubtedly earn you a position of respect. You just have to find your own way first. You have the gentle side of the Maine Coon in you, and that is just as important to our community as many other qualities."

Cream Puff was sure that would never happen—until today. He thought about the last nest of dead kittens he had found after he heard their screams. He had saved a few with furious licking of their mouths, but most were dead before he got there. He felt a furious, deep anger, in a way he had never before.

"What a waste!" he'd snarled, almost running off to follow the scent left by the attacker. As he turned back, he was startled by something moving in the corner of his eye: a huge cat in the window well. He instinctively shrunk away from it, only to see it shrink away from him.

"Wait!" he shouted. "That big cat can't be me!" But frightened cries brought his attention back to kittens; he forgot the attacker—and unbelievable image—as he attended to them.

Cinder and the other community adults sat in a circle after her announcement in the general meeting. They shook their heads and called out solutions, retreating into themselves as they eliminated each idea as too risky or unrealistic. Cream Puff moved closer to the group and sat down as he reached the outside of the circle.

"Ah, can I say something? Please?" One by one, the cats turned towards Cream Puff, who by now was shaking slightly with nerves. "I have a suggestion. Just a suggestion. It'll probably never work but..." His voice trailed off as he lowered his eyes out of respect.

"Yes, Cream Puff?" Cinder said, allowing him an audience.

"Well, what if we have one of the bigger males guard the nest? What if we just did that for a few weeks until the babies were big and smart enough to run away? If there was another attack, this male could get the little ones out of harm's way until the hunting pack came back."

Cinder smiled gently. "But what male would volunteer to do such a menial job. That's usually a female's traditional duty? More importantly, who could we trust with such responsibility? During the long breeding season, these males could be overcome with their hormonal drives!" Cinder sat a little taller; she was proud of her son's intelligent suggestion. Cream Puff moved a little closer to his mother and sister; he was going to need their support for the next part of his plan.

"What if I stayed behind while you all hunted? What if I guarded them? I know I'm not known for my courage and fighting skills, but those young'uns would listen to me. They would run if I told them to—behind the protection of the window well. They trust me!"

"But what if you had to actually fight whatever is doing this, Cream Puff. Could you do that? Even for the kittens' sake?" an elderly ginger-colored female asked, concern etched on her face. "What if you had to defend a kitten against an attack from the sky? What if it was a coyote? Or something even meaner and bigger than you are? Could you defend them—to the death?" she murmured as she moved herself closer.

Cream Puff moved into the center of the circle with confidence he didn't really feel.

"I may not be like the other males; I may not act as aggressive as they do, but I know I have my father's courage, my mother's agility, and my sister's smarts." He thought he saw Furball wink at him and stood a little taller. "I might not be able to save every little one, but what other choices do we have?" His sparkling eyes scanned each cat in the circle, his back straight and his ears and whiskers pointed confidently forward. With sparkling eyes, he surveyed the circle, meeting each one's gaze directly. When he stopped briefly at Cinder, she nodded her head every-so-slightly. "Keep going," she urged when she noticed that the group were silently reflecting on his proposal.

"Let me try. If I fail, I'll step down." His words hung in the air. The elders looked at each other, then at Cinder.

"This," she announced, "is a community decision. Vote as you will. I will agree to whatever you decide. Let me only add that Cream Puff is in the royal line of the long-haired family."

The others wanted to talk alone. With a wide smile of pride, Cinder motioned her son away. He backed away but stayed within calling distance. Within a few minutes, he was summoned back to the center of the circle.

"Okay, Cream Puff," the elderly sister spoke almost in a hush. "We'll give you a chance. But if you are harmed or we continue to lose too many babies, you must agree to another plan."

He lowered his whiskers with respect, while grinning widely at his two favorite felines.

In preparation for his newly-appointed responsibility, Cream Puff behaved very much as he always had. He tumbled in "fun-fights" with the younger kittens, growling in a husky, menacing voice as they lowered for an attack, their little butts shifting in the air from side to side. With the adolescents, he applied more strength and speed to prepare them for future challenges. When a kitten was worn out, it lowered itself onto the sunny steps of the stone house in utter contentment, the tip of its tail slightly flickering. Mesmerized by humming insects and the distant calls of the farm's livestock, he fell into the "alert doze" cats are known for: resting but not actually asleep. Invariably, one of the rested babies couldn't resist stalking his tempting tail as it twitched from side to side...and the tussle was on again! He'd hug the baby as it grabbed his tail and dug into his belly with its hind paws like a tough wrestler. If Cream Puff ignored them, they'd gnaw at his mouth or leg, pestering him into action. Or he might be found covered with dozing kittens with some stretched out by his side or flung on his chest or nuzzled into his furry belly as if he was their mother.

Cream Puff even taught them to "mouse." He'd bring them a weakened mouse one of the hunters was "playing" with from the field, plop it in the middle of the kittens, and show them how to bat at it and then fling it into the air, never allowing it to run far if it escaped. He made it his mission to coach them in the fine arts of fighting, hunting, and killing their food for dinner. All barn cats had to learn to be self-sufficient, even with Leah's generous meals.

One particular sleepy summer day, Cream Puff was being lulled into a doze by the sound of purring kittens. He didn't realize that he was just about to fall asleep when something woke him. Something wasn't right: a distant squeal floated on the wind. Cracking one eye open, he saw a little butterscotch-patched boy walking close to the fence surrounding the pasture. Cream Puff knew that cattle could trample him before he could warn him. At the same time, he spotted a thin, rust-colored animal with oversized, pointed ears edging closer and closer to the unaware kitten.

A fox! The fox family lived across the ravine between the back of the stone house and the forest. They were especially successful hunters, often preying on defenseless kittens.

Without a second's hesitation, Cream Puff sprang into action, leaping over a pile of kittens completely ignorant of the danger so near and sprinting at a speed he had no idea he was capable of.

"Window well! Get to the window well," he screamed as he closed in on the fox, but the kitten was too focused on capturing a meaty grasshopper to hear Cream Puff's desperate warning.

"A fox! Fox! Get back!" Cream Puff cried as he skidded to a stop between the fox and the kitten. "Keep behind me! And don't move!" he hissed at the kitten, slowly backing away from the fox.

Below the fox's sharp snout, a smile formed. Most foxes believe they can outmaneuver even adult cats with their slick movements—especially a cat as cumbersome as this one! Continuing to flash his friendly smile, the fox carefully circled, trying to get behind this bothersome cat to the kitten shrunk into a ball of fear. But no matter how quickly the fox moved, Cream Puff moved even quicker. The hair on Cream Puff's back spiked down his spine, and his fur puffed up like he was inflated, making him look enormous. But more worthy of attention were the razor-sharp teeth bared behind his thin lips. The fox stopped in his tracks; even the craftiest fox had careful respect for those fangs! Ears flattened, Cream Puff weaved and dodged with the fox's every fake dive and charge. His bushy, arched back and brush-like tail threatened until he lunged at the fox with his claws spread like meat hooks. Just for good measure, he let out a piercing and mighty "Yowl!"

Finally, the fox stopped his evil smiling. Thinking wisdom was the better part of valor, it backed slowly away, hopped back to the ravine, and disappeared.

Although scaring off this predator seemed to take hours, the encounter only lasted a few minutes. His fur starting to settle back to his body, Cream Puff gently picked up the shaking kitten by the scruff of its neck and loped back to the farmyard, dropping the naughty little one on the ground. As he began to lecture the kitten about its careless lack of awareness, Cream Puff gradually became aware of whoops of "Hooray for Uncle Puff!" and "Uncle Puff is our hero!" Then the entire crew of wiggling, cheering kittens piled on top of him. Falling exhausted across the step and covered with squealing, squirming kittens, he'd never felt so satisfied with a day's work.

It was only a few days after that encounter when Cream Puff had another challenge, a particularly scary threat. During one sunny summer day, the kittens scattered all over the "safe area" behind the stone house, some chasing grasshoppers and others rolling in play, Cream Puff squinted into the waning sun, beating down its brilliant white.

Again a smoky colored kitten wandered too far from the group, distracted by a monarch butterfly flitting radically around the yard. Cream Puff shook his head in frustration. "Why can't these kids stay close to the window well?"

Slowly sweeping shadows stretched over the yard. In fact, Cream Puff quickly realized there were several circling shadows. Without waiting to identify the shadows, Cream Puff screamed his warning wail, and the kittens dove into the window well. The kittens tucked safely behind the protective wood, he squinted into the sky. Immediately, he discovered a flock of slowly circling turkey vultures, gliding on a current of wind with the grace and beauty of ballerinas. They were no threat. Their job was cleaning up the dead, not killing them for a fresh dinner. But they certainly looked threatening; their wing spans had to be over five feet wide! Again the kittens cried out in praise! "Uncle Puff rescued us again!" "Hurray for Uncle Puff, Protector of Careless Kittens!" as they pounced on him until he was covered in a squirming mass.

"Protecting all you kids sure is hard work." He broke into a wide grin, falling under the weight of so many. "But I sure love you little bits of trouble."

A month later, now late summer, his greatest test came from the sky: a red-tailed hawk silently surveying the farmyard from a huge walnut tree by the side of the stone house. Having flown from the distant woods, it perched in the tree—watching and waiting patiently for a kitten to wander away from the group. Finally, it saw its chance. Effortlessly and without a sound, the bird lifted off and circled the central play area between the barn and the stone house. Cream Puff was preoccupied with the twins, Frick and Frack, laughing at their tumbling all over each other in mock battle, while the others tried to capture the wind through the grasses.

Without a sound, the hawk dove for a bunch of kittens, talons lowered ready to snatch a fresh meal. After the false alarm with the vultures, the kittens often ignored Cream Puff's warnings. But he was too complacent as he dozed to the sound of squeals and giggles. A fast moving shadow alerted him as the sun peeked through a gauze of clouds.

"Enemy in the sky! Run fast!" Cream Puff screamed as he raced for the ball of babies that the hawk was closing in on, screaming a piercing "TSEEAARR."

Cream Puff realized he wouldn't be able to reach them in time, so in the last few feet, he leapt into the air with long, rabbit-like legs and landed right on top of the clutch of kittens.

With an ear-splitting "YOWL," Cream Puff rolled over just as the bird's talons reached to pluck up a kitten. Cream Puff flayed his razor sharp claws in the air just as the bird's talons scraped along his side. He managed to inflict a deep scratch, flinging brown and red feathers in the air. The bird screamed in pain and soared away into the sky.

"Are you kids okay?" Cream Puff yelled as they tried to squirm out from underneath him.

"Uncle Puff, you did it again!" screamed one admiring auburn baby.

"What was that?"

"A giant from the sky!"

"A monster."

"That was no turkey!"

"Boy, you sure are brave, Uncle Puff!" As the rest of kittens started to regroup, Cream Puff winced: a line of crimson seeped from his cream-colored fur.

Just then, Cream Puff heard more screams, this time coming from the across the creek. He looked up to see the returning hunters racing towards the stone house, Cinder in the lead. "Come on ladies!" she urged. "Hurry! The kittens are in trouble." They had heard the kittens' screams and had watched the attack but were too far in the pasture across the creek, too far away to help.

Cinder and Furball sped across the pasture, sailed over the four-foot-wide creek, scrambled up the bank, and raced to the house while the others trailed far behind. When they reached the yard, they pulled the remaining kittens from the prone Cream Puff who was trying to escape from the tangle of bodies.

"Are you okay, brother?" cried Furball frantically.

"I'm fine! Just a scratch!" Cream Puff answered as he scanned his body for the source of the pain. His mother and sister bent to lick at the wound in his side, now a deep crimson, until the red stain faded. When he finally extracted himself from the kittens and their arriving mothers, he shook himself, still quivering from the dangerous attack.

Wanting to appear confident, he declared with false bravado, "All in a day's work."

That night, Cinder assembled the families, asking Cream Puff to sit in the middle of the feline circle. He was afraid he hadn't performed his duty well enough, even though he hadn't lost a single kitten under his protection. He walked awkwardly as he moved to the center, the wound in his side getting sorer with each step.

"I have called this assembly together today," Cinder declared, "because we have witnessed a near tragedy. We could have easily lost our kittens to a red-tail today."

Cream Puff heaved a sigh and lowered his eyes in shame. "Oh boy, I'm in trouble now. I should have been more alert—and quicker," he murmured to himself. He waited for the community to strip him of his guarding duties. "This is going to be more painful than any attack!" he thought glumly.

"But not a single kitten was lost!" Cinder faced her son with that ubiquitous smile on her lips. Even when serious, her congeniality showed through. Even so, Cream Puff braced himself for the inevitable shaming.

"Cream Puff," his mother continued. "Today, we felines saw with our own eyes what our kittens have been bragging about. You have proven yourself brave and conscientious in guarding our most precious assets. We now have many strong kittens to carry on their bloodlines. And it is all because of you!"

Cream Puff's whiskered jaw dropped in surprise as the other cats agreed enthusiastically.

"You have proven yourself to be a true long-haired! In honor of this occasion, we want to commemorate your important contribution to Farmer Bob and Leah's farm. Therefore, son of

Cinder and The Stranger, you are no longer Cream Puff. From today, you will be known as Puff, The Protector." Furball broke into a full smile. The crowd all murmured their agreement: "Mighty Puff!"

"Puff, the Protector!"

In spite of the noisy agreement, several males in the circle shifted uneasily, remembering their taunts towards the cream colored juvenile who played with kittens.

"No more Cream in that Puff!" smiled an elderly, yellow tabby. "You have earned your place in the community."

Puff breathed a very deep sigh of relief as the family circle closed in around him with praise and compliments, nudging agreement. But no one's admiration meant more to him than the kittens who wiggled through and under the adults to smother him with cheers of "Uncle Puff, The Protector!"

His side didn't even hurt any more. He had proven his worth. And Puff had a war wound to prove he'd won the prize he was after: protector of the cats and his community for generations to come.

Puff: Protector of the Kittens

CHAPTER 4

Hunter Arrives

"WHO IS THIS INTRUDER?" THOUGHT FURBALL She had just returned from an afternoon of hunting when she saw the strange cat sluggishly working its way across the mounds of sloppy, spring mud in the driveway, heading towards the stone house.

"What kind of trouble might this mean?" Furball whispered to herself. As alpha, she often had to make quick decisions that would affect the entire community. She was wise in seeking opinions of other adult cats, but ultimately it was her decision.

The alpha pricked up her ears, her sweeping whiskers stretched forward in order to sense everything possible from this stranger. "Oh great! She's pregnant!" Furball lamented. "And soon ready too!"

The bulging, otherwise thin cat deliberately picked her way up the driveway in a hesitant zig-zag path. Looking around with wide, hazel eye, the cat struggled up the steep-walled ruts left by the trucks and cars. She was a short-hair with a blend of orange and black, mixed in with some white spots like a homemade quilt. She worked to move at all, walking in an unnatural gait. Her huge belly made progress very slow. Finally slowing down to a stop, she seemed unsure of whether to go forward or retreat when Furball loped down the driveway, making herself known to the intruder.

"Well, what do we have here?" asked Furball. She wore no smile on her face, but her tone wasn't hostile either. "Before you go any further, you need to understand this is the private cattle farm of Mr. Farmer Bob and Leah. You are now on the property of Queen Cinder's feline community. As reigning alpha, I am the guardian of this farm…" She paused to see if the stranger was paying attention. "And we have no need of any outsiders! Move on," she warned.

Avoiding direct eye contact, the foreign cat looked down at the ground between them. She slowly lowered herself into a semi-crouch with her bulbous stomach and kept her eyes on the ground.

"I come as no enemy but come to this farm out of necessity. I am ready to birth my first litter," she explained, barely able to catch her breath. "I have wandered a long way for a place to rest. And I saw your barn. I need some dry hay and some protection of some—sort—just for their birthing." She hesitated, briefly sneaking a peak at Furball. "I will move them off the farm as soon as they open their eyes." She paused again for a breath. "And it will be soon!"

The pregnant cat then looked directly at the alpha, her eyes searching Furball's very soul.

Furball leaned forward a little. Sometimes smells communicate messages in the animal kingdom. But she could only pick up field smells: newly sprouted weeds along with last winter's dead grasses.

"I really need help," the calico cat pled.

Still no answer. Furball kept her silence.

"When they are born, I won't ask for any help. I can feed them myself; I am the most expert hunter! I promise I will be no trouble. I just need a dry place to have my kittens."

Sensing the alpha's resolve, she rose, ready to depart, shifting her heavy weight onto her back feet and turning in the direction she'd come.

"Wait! I make decisions with the advice of the cat elders. Stay here. I will discuss your situation with my community when they're back from their chores and hunting." Furball slowly backed away, knowing this cat was no threat but also knowing the strong survival urges of a soon-to-be mother.

Exhaling a deep sigh, the other cat relaxed for the first time. She stayed in her place with her front paws neatly placed side-by-side. Her sides moved in waves like wheat in a passing wind. But she stayed put. Much depended on her stance and eye contact; she had to do everything she could to show cooperation and respect. She clearly understood she was an outsider!

Furball headed up to the community meeting spot next to the stone house in between big, round hay bales and rusting farm implements. As the cats arrived, they couldn't help but notice Furball wore her "This is important" look: ears and whiskers alert, a serious expression in her eyes.

The elders formed a circle around her, with the families of cats behind them. Everyone murmured with excitement when they saw the unfamiliar, bulbous cat seated down the long driveway.

"We have a wanderer seeking safe harbor for her soon-to-be-with-us kittens. She has asked to stay here until the kittens can be moved, soon after they are born, I would hope." She paused for the right words. "My own opinion is mostly driven by my own experience as a mother. I feel for her." Again she paused, carefully choosing her words. "However, we must be very diligent and careful about refugee cats who appear on the farm. Newcomers can mean serious danger to our close-knit community."

Furball's daughter, a black beauty named Bear, scowled.

"Although you've already had your kittens, I just had my first litter. We really don't have time and room for another bunch of newborns, especially given all the attacks we've had recently. We just can't protect all of the kittens!" She shook her head and ruffled her cascading, raven-colored fur. "We don't need more mouths to feed. This is no time to take on more responsibility"

Although a reasonable argument against accepting the mother cat, Furball was somewhat surprised by her daughter's harsh resistance. While she agreed with Bear, forcing this new family to leave a safe farm for dangers of the wilderness was not in her nature.

"But we must also remember that we are all descendants of The Stranger. He was an outsider too. We owe our very existences to his brief stay here." Furball stared at her daughter with liquid eyes. "How should we treat this one when we owe so much?"

"Still—I don't trust those from the outside; they can mean trouble. Bad trouble. It is a dilemma! What do the rest of you say?" Furball was faced with a problem with no certain solution. Was not an individual's welfare equally as important as that of the community? A wrong decision could bring disaster. Yet hospitality could mean good fortune. It could go either way.

Furball stepped back from the center of the circle and waited. Yellow Kitty, a large male tabby and a close friend to Furball, spoke first. "We, of course, will abide by your decision as our leader, but as long as she's no threat, I think we can easily afford the space and food for her—temporarily, of course."

How she loved the sweet nature and voice of reason of these yellow tabbies. The two cats often sunned themselves on the hood of Farmer Bob's truck after dinner. When resting, she'd rub against him, snuggling against him, murping softly. They liked to work together on hunts. She'd always favored Yellow Kitty. These yellows made the best fathers for her kitten families: good strong genetic material and wonderful caretakers of their young.

"I disagree," interrupted Bear passionately. "Maybe the threat will come much later. We must be vigilant! Now!"

"I agree with Yellow Kitty," echoed Puff, The Protector. He knew first-hand what it felt like to be ostracized by other cats.

Hunter Arrives

"We mustn't turn out a mother—especially with newborns. Maybe ask her to leave when she and her brood are ready."

"Your opinions are all well-meaning, Mother," Cinnamon, another of Furball's daughters, offered, "but we have our own kittens to think of too, and this cat could mean a serious challenge to the community, to our family, the long-hairs! It's too risky!" All the cats yowled in noisy agreement and dissent.

"You all have good points!" Furball shouted to quiet them. She waited, pawing absentmindedly at the muddy ground in front of her.

"How about this? We could set apart one of the bays of the barn to make a temporary home for her family. She would not ever mix her kittens with ours, and we'd have the larger, more sheltered bay on the east. But—she must abide by some conditions first." Cinnamon sat down, apparently satisfied that she had been heard. Her mother continued. "She and her offspring must never challenge the long-haired line and certainly not our alpha. The shorthairs will always be subordinate to us. Her kittens must in every way keep their distance! We will keep them separated by the empty bay between us!

"Next, they should never venture down to the stone house where the humans feed us. In fact, they must never have anything to do with our humans! That is solely our privilege.

"Finally, if they ever challenge the alpha's authority, they are out! Period!"

Furball was as generous as her mother, Cinder, but she was much more protective of her cat community in general. She never knew her father. He was an unknown, and so was this mystery cat.

"If she will agree to this contract, we will give her shelter." The others nodded their approval of these arrangements. Furball loped down the driveway and approached the very uncomfortable cat waiting for her fate to be announced. Again, she stared at the ground and listened closely to the community's requirements.

"Do you agree to the terms just explained," asked Furball.

"I do," the cat replied.

"OK, then the cream-colored cat, Puff, The Protector, will show you to the shed." The cats all watched as Puff escorted the waddling cat in his gentle way.

Late that afternoon, the soon-to-be mother tunneled deep into the square bales of musty hay. The breeze from across the creek cooled the bay while the afternoon sun warmed it. "Perfect accommodations," she murmured.

As she reviewed the events since struggling up the hill to confront the alpha, she reflected on how impressed she was with Furball's handling of the situation and the compassion in letting a stranger remain on the farm. She had not heard Furball's defense, but she had noted the gentleness in her expression, especially her soft eyes as she stated the conditions of the contract. Furball even seemed to imply that this might work into a permanent home if the stranger and her family faithfully maintained their secondary status. The short hairs were the "other" family and that arrangement must never change!

As she lay in the fading twilight, she felt a tightening of her abdomen. It was starting. Just in time.

The calico mother was a strong cat, wiry but with strong muscles. Each of her kittens turned out healthy and hungry; even the runt nursed eagerly at its first feeding. The very next morning, the new mother was up, leaving the tangled mass of squirming kittens to search for mice, usually abundant in the hay. After again nursing the mass of pink mouths, she felt compelled to leave them to join the other hunters for the afternoon hunt.

She kept her distance and disappeared into the distant part of the field, to hunt alone. She returned in less than an hour with a sizable young rabbit, proudly carrying it to her nest in the hay. After filling her stomach with much needed nourishment, she nursed the restless kittens again and finally found a quiet moment to rest.

Oh, how she hoped this place could become "home."

Although she knew she had no business near the others, she left the meatiest part of the rabbit in front of the far bay before the others returned from hunting. In spite of her violation of the contract by not keeping herself separated, Furball was impressed with this prompt offering of gratitude. From that time on, if the hunt did not produce enough food for the ever growing community, they could depend on this "other" sharing in her abundance.

Many days later, one of the calico's kittens stumbled out of the bay; its eyes had just opened.

"Where is its mother?" Cinnamon wondered as she passed the bay. "A curious kitten means danger," she ominously warned, leaning close to the ground to be heard. "You're going to be the adventurous one, aren't you?"

The tiny dark calico tried to focus on the taller cat with full, moon-like eyes.

Cinnamon had to smile in spite of herself and nosed it gently, aiming it back into the bay. "With those big, round eyes, your name should be Dianna, the name that Leah uses for the moon sometimes." Assuming this to be its mother, it mewed hungrily and pushed its tiny nose into the big cat's sturdy legs. Knowing it couldn't understand, Cinnamon lifted it gently by its neck skin, went to the far bay, and deposited it in the nest with the rest of its littermates. The kitten protested loudly at which point its mother raced into the shed.

Expecting the residents' usual disapproval, she edged almost sideways toward the nest, careful not to look directly into Cinnamon's eyes. But Cinnamon stepped away, indicating she meant no harm and smiled! There was no physical interaction between the two females, just mutual esteem for the many responsibilities of motherhood.

Still, the new mother kept her distance from the others. She didn't trust the rest of the community, even after her interaction with Cinnamon. And she certainly didn't trust the humans, so she and her family rarely appeared in public. Leah might spy them out in the tall grass or roaming around in the bay, but the community never communicated with or were even seen near the calico.

Within a month of the "other" cat's arrival, Furball and the others met while she was off hunting. The babies now had their eyes completely open and were venturing closer to the forbidden bays and the stone house every day. Furball knew they had to decide quickly about moving them off their property.

"What should we do?" she asked the group circled around her.

Cinnamon focused on the ground and then spoke first. "This mother cat has proven herself. She is a good provider, a great hunter, and she respects our community. And the kittens mostly have obeyed the rules too." She smiled to herself, remembering the day Dianna mistook her for her mother. "I vote for allowing her to stay. Permanently."

Furball smiled approvingly at her daughter. Puff and Yellow Kitty bobbed their heads in agreement. Although not whole-heartedly, even Bear seemed satisfied with the proposal. It was settled. The family could stay as long as they continued to abide by the rules of the contract.

One evening near dusk, Leah and Farmer Bob were resting in front of the stone house after a hard day's work before they headed back to their home in the city. The flying insects dived and soared around the porch light. Cicadas and frogs, along with occasional cattle, sang their songs of evening rest.

"Ya know, Leah," commented Farmer Bob. "I haven't seen a single rat this year. You think it's that new cat?"

Just at that very moment, the calico cat appeared in the cone of light swarming with mesmerized insects. Then, with a six-foot high leap as graceful as a trapeze artist, she effortlessly plucked a moth out of the air. She tucked the bug tightly in her mouth with her front paws and disappeared into the corner of the bay. She glanced back at the couple as if she were allowing them to witness her feats of agility.

"Wow! She's a fantastic jumper. With such accuracy too! That moth didn't have a chance. The other day, I watched her pluck an unsuspecting bird right out of the air!!! Like it was nothing!"

She smiled with admiration. "I think we should call her 'Hunter'?"

Hunter and her family soon became important, contributing members of the community.

CHAPTER 5

Bear

THE WEATHER HAD TAKEN A DRASTIC TURN FOR THE WORSE. A combination of below freezing temperatures, unending snow, and blasting winds swept away any warmth provided by the lemon-yellow sun to the cats on the farm. The cattle surrounded a huge hay bale, trying to position themselves so they either faced the sun or the opposite side of the driving wind, eating with their heads in and back ends out. During the severe weather, Leah was more attentive than usual to the cats, especially the smaller ones. She often checked the huddled bodies in the window well near the door of the stone house or burrowed deep in the loosened hay, forming a tightly woven clump of warmth like a ball of multicolored yarn.

"Where is Bear?" Leah whispered in a frosted cloud. "She hasn't come for food. Now that I think about it, I haven't seen her since last weekend!" When Leah asked Farmer Bob if he had seen the cat, he said that he hadn't seen her in days either.

So Leah started to hunt, checking the window well, in the barrels at the end of shed, in the stacks of hay, under the feed trough, and in all of the cats' other favorite sheltered places.

She found no traces of the cat. No Bear was to be found!

Like most of the other long-hairs in her clan, Bear had a stocky build and flowing mane, but she had no color, covered in a sea of black fur. And in spite of her clan's alpha status, Bear was never much interested in assuming a dominant role; she was completely content to leave that responsibility up to Furball.

Neither did she have her mother's and siblings' athleticism or competitive nature. But being unusually heavy for a farm cat, she lumbered in a slow-motion stroll, her body shifting from side to side when she walked, unlike the fluid movement of the other members of her clan.

"Like a bear!" Leah laughed. "You look just like a little black bear cub. You will be our 'Bear.'"

However, she did have the long-hairs' social nature. So she always sought out Leah to be held and petted, and Leah reciprocated with some special care and scratches around her mane. Bear was Leah's favorite. So when the cat was not present for food or pets, Leah's concern quickly bordered on desperation.

After searching the entire day for her, Leah was tempted to give up, recognizing the hard facts of the farm cats' difficult existence. She knew she had to be a realist. Their cats often died in the harsh winters despite all her and Farmer Bob's care, but she felt responsible for them all. And especially loved her missing friend.

As the day inched towards dusk, Leah finally resigned herself. Bear, she thought, must be dead. Dragging her feet in the deep snow, she wandered to the stone house to start dinner for the rest of the cats. Just as she stepped on the landing, she noticed something out of the corner of her eye: a black puddle on the frozen snow on top of a barrel by the east bay. Bear had apparently come out from her shelter to try to warm herself in the waning sun.

"Bear! It's Bear! Oh Bob, come here!" Leah screamed as she ran to her beloved companion. Her body lay limp in the last of the afternoon sun, a huge frozen cyst on her chest from her waist to her collar bone, covering half of her body. The surrounding skin and fur were frozen hard as the stone house.

Farmer Bob gasped when he joined her.

"It looks like she has been bitten by something awful, maybe a male cat who tried to breed her." He bent over to examine the cat more closely, quickly determining that she was hardly breathing, too near death to take to the vet.

But Leah refused to give up. So she immediately carried Bear into the stone house and warmed some food. But Bear wouldn't eat. She did drink huge amounts of warm water. In spite of her fur thawing, Leah's efforts seemed to be of no use.

Seeing how hard Leah was working to save Bear, Farmer Bob suggested, "What about seeing what the vet says?" Leah carefully wrapped her up. Bear gave no resistance; she was too numb and weak to care.

At the vet's, the doctor, a recent graduate with a crown of blond braids, tenderly examined her.

"I'll try to get some intravenous liquids into her now and clean up the wound as best as I can. She's so weak and has a fever. If she doesn't eat, she won't survive. Leah—Bob," she whispered to them, "I wouldn't hold out much hope for her survival. But I'll try. You will have to force-feed her with this long-nosed syringe. She isn't resisting now, but if she gets any stronger, you might have to wrap a towel around her to hold her while you feed her. Several times a day."

As the antique wall clock slowly ticked a peaceful tempo, the cat lay still on the cold, metallic examining table. As they worked and whispered over her, Bear shivered, sighed deeply and often slowly glanced sideways at Leah.

I wish they'd let me alone, so I can pass over, she thought. *I can't stand this pain— or Leah's sad face—anymore.*

"If she lives for the next two or three days, she might eventually be okay. After a week or so, the cyst and all the dead skin will fall off. Don't be concerned for how it looks when that happens. Eventually all the skin and hair will grow back." She hesitated, glancing at the shrunken spot of black, and then turned to the humans. "If any farmers in this county can save her, it's the two of you."

On their way back to their home in the city, Leah held the bone-thin cat closely to her to keep her warm. This was Bear's first ride in a vehicle, but she was too weak to care about this strange trip. The only thing she responded to were the street and car lights, tracking them with wonder in her eyes.

What are those huge shooting stars all around us? she wondered. *Maybe this is the other side for us cats. The pain seems a little less.*

The cat's attention to the lights gave Leah hope.

When they arrived home, Leah placed her in the bathroom: small enough to limit her activity and warmer than the rest of the house. Leah covered the floor with newspaper and set the box of litter in the bath tub. Then she carefully placed Bear in the tub on the softest fleece blanket she could find.

"I don't even know if she will use the litter, but we are doing the best we can for her, Leah. Let's let her be for now," Farmer Bob quietly suggested.

When they left, Bear moaned as she shifted her body. The pain shot through her like lightning through a black sky. It was as if she were waking from a nightmare. *Oh, what is happening? I don't remember anything but cold and pain. The cold is gone, but not the pain.*

Wincing, Bear slowly pulled herself to a sitting position, holding her breath. Panting from the exertion, she let her body fall back on the blanket. *Where am I now? It doesn't smell like the farm at all. And no whistling wind or cattle complaining of the cold. Where is my family? Where are all the other cats? Where is Mother?* Soon her breathing slowed as she gave in to sleep.

Bear was startled awake when Leah quietly entered the bathroom the next day to find the cat had not moved from the blanket. For those first days, Leah force-fed her every six hours and left yogurt in a ceramic bowl in case she could eat. Bear hardly resisted at all but simply had no strength to eat the yogurt.

Then on the third morning, Leah was so relieved to find that the cat had eaten the entire bowl of yogurt. For the first time since finding Bear near death, Leah breathed freely, hoping that she just might survive after all.

Within a week, Bear was eating every bit of food and starting to explore the bathroom. When Leah entered the bathroom, the cat would greet her at the door and lie on her back to get rubbed. Eventually the dead skin and cyst fell off; the wound was slowly shrinking as it healed from the edges inward.

"She looks so much better," said Leah to her friend Beth, a short woman with flyaway, curly hair colored with salty accents, after a few weeks of "hospital care" in the bathroom. "It's still a bad wound," Leah said as she scrunched Bear under her chin, "but you're eating so well! And you even meet me when I come in, just like at the farm. Bear, you remember my friend, Beth, from her visits to the farm? She wanted to see my brave girl."

Beth stood still until Bear moved towards her and rubbed against her affectionately. "After what you've been through, I'm very impressed with your determination to live!" she said, reaching down to pet the cat. "I know some humans who could take a lesson from you, Bear."

"I know you're not ready for the farm yet," Leah continued. "You need more time in a clean, warm place, but you must be getting bored in this tiny bathroom, so we're going to take you to Beth's house where you'll have more space."

"I have a home with a big basement, Bear. And I have a surprise for you: one of your sisters. Remember Angel? It really hasn't been that long since she left the farm and came to live with me in town. She would love to see you."

Bear gazed at Leah and Beth, her eyes almost winking at them as if she understood every word. She continued to weave between the legs of the two women, rumbling deep-throated purrs of contentment.

"It'll be just a little while. Until you are stronger and the wound heals. It'll be fun for you and Angel to get reacquainted. And think about how you can brag to the others at the farm that you not only survived, but saw your sister, too! Furball will be so pleased," Leah assured her.

After they left, Bear finished off the hard food in her bowl, swiping her chin with her paws, and waited for whatever was going to happen. She didn't know exactly what Leah was talking about, not understanding language, but she felt reassured by Leah's calm voice and Beth's rubs in her favorite spots.

Well, something is about to happen, and it sounded like something good.

A few days later, Leah wrapped Bear in a warm blanket and carried her to the car. Within a short time, she was in another strange place like the bathroom but warmer and much larger. And it had some great shadowy corners and hidden spaces to explore. Leah placed her on something soft and puffy and orange that contoured to her body.

"This, Bear, is where I will do my paper work every evening," Beth explained. "But you're welcome to sit with me."

When Leah and Beth left, Bear stayed on the "orange puff" for awhile until she felt confident enough to slide to the floor and explore the basement. She found a box of small pebbles that invited her to use it as a toilet: strange but effective. The basement was divided into two rooms—one with thin carpeting where the "orange puff" resided, and the other with a slippery floor. This second room emitted a constant hum and then suddenly erupted into a loud moaning sound. When Bear first heard it, she was so terrified she hid under the "orange puff."

"It's only the furnace," Beth told her. "It'll keep you warm." Whatever that is, thought Bear, it sounds like Farmer Bob's tractor that he moves hay with, growling on and off. But this thing, this "furnace," never moves. Eventually she approached it, but she always kept a safe distance. It took a lot of courage to even do that.

But on the positive side, there were bugs to chase and eat in the basement and dark crevices with strands of wispy webs that caught in her whiskers. Just like on the farm. And it's a lot more exciting than that tub! But the best part is the "orange puff" where I sink in, curl up, and drift off to sleep. This must be what it feels like on a cloud in the sky.

Often she could hear muffled sounds above her and thumps that marched across the ceiling. With courage and with usual feline curiosity, she couldn't help climbing the steep stairs to a landing before a tightly shut door. A thin shaft of light crept under the door like a layer of white snow. Beth was talking to someone in a hurried voice.

"She's downstairs, but you can talk with her under the door."

The next day after Beth left, Bear again climbed the stairs to the landing before the closed door. Curiosity drove her to paw tentatively at the door, making muffled scrapes, and then to reach as far as her paw and front leg could go under the door.

Nothing.

Then she tried to reach all along the width of the door, spreading her paw wide to grasp whatever was on the other side.

"Meow?" Bear called out.

Still nothing.

Discouraged, she was just about to give up when she heard a slight disturbance coming from the other side of the door. A muffled breathing. A presence!

She held her breath. Then, gradually, a paw appeared under the door, like her own but with shadowy gray stripes. It searched the width of the door, reaching with outstretched claws, touching the floor and then swiping the door itself in short pats. Then it withdrew.

    Is that another cat? Bear wondered. Didn't Beth mention something about another cat from the farm living with her? But what if it's a dog, our arch enemy? How will I know if it is friendly or dangerous? I'm so scared but very curious! And I am so lonely. Wouldn't it be great if it is another cat?

    Bear tentatively answered the stranger with her own paw, sniffing to try and identify this stranger. Her ears perked up straight when she heard breathing with short sniffs of air followed by a muffled "Merp?"

    The call somehow seemed vaguely familiar.

    "Merp!" she answered. Something was different but recognizable as the two sniffed and breathed and pawed at each other under the door. It sounds like a cat and smells like a cat. But it might not be a friendly cat!

    This "communication" continued for many days, each time lasting longer and involving more interaction. They even played "pawsies" with each other, touching and grasping the other's paw under the door.

    Beth spent most evenings on the "orange puff" with a confused mess of paper work while watching the small TV. Each night she climbed the stairs and closed the door at the top with a click. Several nights later, Bear thought she heard the door shut but with no click of the doorknob. So she slowly inched paw by paw up the stairs to a lighted room, the door left open like an invitation.

    "Hey, Bear," Beth called. "Welcome to the kitchen. Come on in, Bear," she cooed. The brightness was almost unbearable, similar to the light on the side of the stone house that was so bright none of the cats could look directly into it.

    She slowly emerged from the stairs and crept step-by-careful-step under the protective table and chairs, under a table with wheels, and finally to the adjoining room.

The smells there were entirely foreign to a barn cat, but, for some reason, they made her mouth water. Beth turned off the bright lights and disappeared down a long hallway, snapping the door shut, so that Bear was left to explore the house by herself for the rest of the night, punctuated by shafts of light coming in from the outside. It took a long time to cover all the rooms until she was exhausted from exploring and trundled stair-by-stair down to the "orange puff" to think about what she'd discovered. That was exciting. Scary but exciting! I wonder where the noisy "presence" was? I wonder what it is. I'll find out tomorrow.

The next day, she awoke with a start to find that "presence" nearly on top of her. It was another cat, staring and sniffing at her. But, somehow, this "presence" was so familiar! Looking at it was a little like seeing her own image looking back at her in the reflective window of the window well.

"I know you're the presence, but who are you?" Bear ventured as she slowly rose and backed away, her hair standing straight up. That was when she noticed Beth was watching them. Bear was tempted to hiss at the other cat, but since they had already "talked" several times under the door, there was no need for aggression. Yet.

"I know who I am. But who are you and what are you doing in my basement?" demanded the other cat, her magnificently long whiskers twitching, her eyes so dark they looked like she wore black mascara. Her ruff of long, cascading hair circled her neck—just like Bear's.

"You know, you look just like my mother, Furball," Bear observed.

"And you smell like the farm where I came from. And my mother was called 'Furball' too," shouted the other cat. "Do you know Leah and Farmer Bob?"

"They live on my farm!" Bear exclaimed.

"Oh, my stars-in-the-sky, my name is Angel! I'm your sister! You must be Bear!"

Bear started to circle Angel and rub up against her. Angel instantly purred in response.

"How is Mother? And the rest of the family? And how is Farmer Bob? Do you guys still catch mice in the hay? And ride the rafters? Tell me all about the farm! Don't leave out one detail," Angel demanded as the two followed Beth up the stairs.

The rest of the afternoon the two talked and touched and sniffed and laughed at their mutual memories of kittenhood. That evening, the two slept on the soft quilt at the bottom of Beth's bed, lying over and around each other with limbs tucked into each other's fur, tangled in a ball—just like back at the farm.

As the days passed, Angel showed Bear her favorite places and shared her favorite adventures.

"Let me show you the best fun game ever," Angel said. "It's called 'Spot the Spider.' You begin by examining the walls for any unusual, moving spot." Angel demonstrated by sitting in front of a wall and slowly scanning its surface in front of her. After a few minutes, she spotted something inching its way down the wall. As it came closer, she dropped into a crouch and froze. Sure enough, when the spider came within range, Angel swiped it up before it even had a chance to dart away.

"Wow!" Bear exclaimed. "Hey, let's go down to the basement. There are hundreds of crawling things down there. Oh, and what is that growly box down there that sounds like Farmer Bob's tractor?"

"Oh, that's a furnace; it keeps us warm!"

By the time they were finished playing in the basement, their whiskers were covered in dangling, delicate webs that clung to their smiles.

"Now let's explore the pipes," Angel suggested, so they

took turns climbing from the two huge boxes that churned and swished, up to the window ledges, and then to the rusty, flaking pipes that disappeared into the wall.

"Doesn't this remind you of the rafters at the farm?"

"Yeah! Only warmer! And slippery," giggled Bear.

The two spent hours playing games and sharing stories about their kittenhood together. Bear told about the attack that almost killed her and how she came to travel from the farm to Leah's house to Beth's house. She even let Angel gently lap at her wound.

At night, they slept on the "orange puff" or on Beth's quilt, draped over each other just like they did as kittens in Furball's nest at the farm. The pair became sisters again.

After what seemed days and days and days, Leah arrived to visit with Beth. "Bear, you look so strong now!" she murmured to Bear as she cuddled her to her chest. "Don't you think it is time to go home?"

Bear knew what Leah was saying, that, sadly, it was time she returned home, but she also knew it meant saying good-bye to Angel. When Leah let Bear down on the kitchen floor, Angel slowly rubbed along her side and licked her between her ears and down her face.

"We knew this would eventually happen, Sis." Angel hesitated, unable to talk. Looking down at the floor, she continued. "But I will miss you! Terribly!" She looked up into her sister's eyes. "Tell everyone I am safe and happy here with Beth, but that I miss them all too. Especially Mother."

As the two gave each other final rubs and licks, Bear said, "Thanks, Angel, for everything! It was so great seeing my sister again!"

"I'll remember our special visit for a long, long time," purred Angel. "Maybe we will meet again for a longer one. I love you, Sister Bear!"

As Leah carried Bear on her shoulder out the door, Bear smiled broadly at Angel and shouted, "Keep the pipes clean!"

That night, Bear cautiously emerged from Farmer Bob's car at the farm and walked all over the place, sniffing and checking out the barn, the stone house, the creek, and the shed.

"I recognize this place," she said to herself, "but it still feels strange somehow. And those cats smell funny! In fact, they stink!"

She kept away from the other cats as it took some time to feel comfortable with them again. They likewise kept their distance from her. Certainly, they thought, Bear had returned from the dead! Furball, though, was especially elated to have her daughter home again, whether from a distant place or the dead. She sniffed Bear from the tip of her nose to tip of her tail before vigorously rubbed her chin and whiskers against Bear in loving welcome. Gradually, Bear shared all about her adventures in the house in the city with Angel.

"Now Bear," Furball said, cocking her head in disbelief, "are you sure you did all that? And that there is such a place as this city? And seeing your sister?" But when Bear described Angel, who resembled Furball more than any of her other kittens, and related their identical histories, their mother beamed a knowing smile and lowered her head in deep thought.

"I couldn't make all this up. And Angel wanted me to tell you how she loves and misses everyone—especially you!" Bear twitched her tail and smiled the long-hairs' smile at the memories of her time in the city. With her sister. Playing "Spot the Spider" and sleeping on the "orange puff."

Often at the end of the day when the sun begins to hide behind the corn fields, Bear gazes into the horizon. She sends thoughts to her sister far beyond the fading sun, knowing that, somehow, the sun was in the city too. Maybe Angel's looking at that same sunset right now out of the window near the growling furnace, she thinks. Bear relaxes into the prickly hay and imagines the softness of the "orange puff," Angel's legs wrapped around her as she drifts into a deep sleep where she and Angel play together again.

CHAPTER 6

Furball's Death and Funeral

THE DEEP WINTER DAY WAS GRAY. Thin layers of dingy clouds smothered the farm like a blanket, hiding the sun that could have provided some heat. This winter was the most severe the cats could remember. The temperature was so low the landscape itself had cracked. The frozen creek groaned under the weight of thick ice.

The cats spent much of their time seeking shelter protected from at least the wind that made the freezing cold that much colder. The hay bales and window wells were their favorite refuges, but this winter was so bitter, many of the cats squeezed themselves into the wheel wells of cars that parked beside the stone house. The warmth there was intense, heat radiating from the recently turned-off engine. Not all the cats could fit into the tire wells, so they gathered on top of the hood. Furball, being alpha, had first bid on the choice wheel wells as a privilege of that status.

"I'm going to warm myself in the wheel well of Farmer Bob's truck," Furball called to the other cats after breakfast. "I won't be gone long, just until I get the chill out of my bones."

"Be careful, Mother. Remember to run when Farmer Bob starts up the truck and blows the horn," warned Bear.

"Don't worry about this alpha!" responded Furball, obviously irritate with her daughter's boldness. Realizing Bear's concern was out of love, not disrespect, she softened her tone. "Sure, Bear, I'll be careful."

With that, Furball carefully squeezed herself into a still-warm, dark well covered with dirt and grime from the road. She hunkered down on a clean, snowless spot on the tire and rested in the fading warmth. Soon she was purring softly as she dozed.

She didn't hear the crunch of Farmer Bob's heavy boots in the snow. She didn't hear his call: "All cats. Off the wheels!" She did feel the starting of the engine and the rumble of the truck. But Furball assumed he was just warming up the truck. She settled back down, knowing she would hear the horn before he drove off, giving her plenty of time to run to safety.

But Farmer Bob wasn't warming the truck and forgot to honk the horn. By the time he'd backed the truck down the ruts in the driveway, it was too late. The wheel had crushed her body without mercy. She lay limp in the snow, bleeding from her mouth, motionless. "Furball! What have you done?" Farmer Bob cried when he saw her. He threw open the door and lumbered through the piles of snow into the tire tread tracks where he could move more quickly. When he reached the lifeless cat, he knelt and lifted her carefully. He knew immediately there was no hope.

"Oh, Furball! You of all cats know better! Why didn't you run?"

He stroked her with gentle hands, hoping against hope, to feel some life and maybe to revive her. But her body was limp. She wasn't breathing. He knew it was futile.

"Oh, what am I going to tell Leah? What am I going to tell her? Oh, Furball, you should have run, my girl!"

As Farmer Bob headed towards the stone house, Leah came out the door and saw her husband cradling Furball in his arms. Momentarily, she froze as she realized the gravity of the scene.

"Oh, Furball," she cried. "Oh, Furball. Our alpha!" Leah held the cat to her chest, oblivious to the cold and the darkening sky that threatened more snow.

"Oh, Leah, I'm so sorry. I forgot to honk the horn. She should have run. But she stayed and…"

"Bob, you can't blame yourself. Furball knew it was dangerous. My poor Furball!"

"We can't leave her until tomorrow," Farmer Bob said, eyeing the threat of coming snow in the dark sky. "We have to bury her now."

"Oh, maybe she isn't dead…maybe she isn't really gone. Maybe if we give her some time," Leah pleaded.

"Leah," Farmer Bob said, looking into her eyes, "just hold her while I dig a hole for her." He lowered the two onto the top step of the stone house and headed towards the creek where a huge oak hung to the bank.

By now, all the cats in the area knew something unusual had happened. All the community circled Leah and their fallen alpha. Blue Eyes moved closer, sniffed Furball's still warm body, licked gently at her mouth, and then moved up to her ears.

"Oh, Mother. I warned you!" groaned Bear as she slowly licked her. "Mother, Don't go! Not yet. Please!"

But it was no use.

One by one, the cats lowered their heads in silence.

Leah rocked the dead cat. "What will we ever do without you?" she moaned into her fur. "You were the best alpha. The best ever!" Finally noticing all the cat community huddled around her, Leah lowered Furball to her lap. The long-haired daughters and sons, grand kittens, and even Hunter and Dianna moved closer.

"What's wrong with Grandma?" asked a tabby kitten. "Why doesn't she get up?"

Bear moved as close as she could to the tabby's side. "Grandma had a horrible accident. She stayed in the wheel well when Farmer Bob moved the truck. The wheels crushed her."

"But why doesn't she move?"

"There are times when we cats aren't careful enough... and other things happen that we have very little control over, like our enemies the fox and red-tailed hawk. Life here on the farm can be dangerous. Remember when you almost drowned in the creek as a kitten? You were supposed to wait for an adult to help you across, but you didn't. Luckily, the current took you only a short distance until you were able to scramble to shore." Bear paused as she searched for words she knew Furball would have known.

"You must learn from this. You must never forget our grief and pain because our leader, our grandmother has died. You must always look for danger. Always!" she whispered with a new urgency.

"But where is she? And who took her from us?" the cat insisted.

"Well, young one, humans call the end of life for animals the 'Rainbow Bridge.' The bridge takes every animal to the next stage of existence." The young cat wrinkled its brow, twitched its whiskers, and crouched with its elbows protruding from its body like cricket legs.

"We cats don't know how or when we must leave this life, but we believe that we live on, whether we simply cross over a bridge, like over our creek, or in some way arrive at a new existence. We believe it's a place with no enemies or sadness or need to hunt for food. Sort of like summer all the time with no freezing winters and predators."

Bear stared at her mother's body as her cobalt eyes moistened.

"I don't know if there are humans there, but we believe that Furball and others who have gone before us will greet our Leah and Farmer Bob when they are ready to 'cross over.'"

"But this place...how do we know it's real?"

"We don't know. No cat has ever returned. We believe in it."

Bear stared at Furball. She knew she wasn't explaining herself very well.

"Will I go there too?" the kitten asked. "Can I go there right now and find Grandma?"

"Oh, no. We never know when we will move on. It could happen any time, or it could happen years from now. But let's not worry about that right now; we have enough to worry over already."

Bear inched closer to the kitten, licking and purring softly into its ears. The kitten closely watched as each cat in turn approached Furball, sniffing or licking her. He tried his best to understand all this new information. The "Rainbow Bridge?" A place where all cats go but can never return.

"Come now! All cats," Bear called. "We must follow Leah to the grave." According to the rights of inheritance, Bear was the new alpha. She knew she had to take up the role of leader immediately, so she started down to the creek.

Leah picked up Furball and headed across the rock-hard ground to the creek's edge. She huddled around the cat as if to keep her warm and rolled her in a tightly wrapped shroud of clean towels. She approached the gnarled, huge oak next to the creek where Farmer Bob had dug a small grave. This area was a peaceful place where kittens loved to play hide-and-seek in the exposed roots and crevices of the cottonwood—a perfect burial site for their beloved alpha.

The cats followed Leah to the tree in crooked lines of various hues and sizes, both clans gingerly weaving their way over frozen creek, a multi-colored ribbon waving in a gentle breeze. The cats formed a circle of mourners with Furball's immediate family in front, sitting formally with front paws together as they waited for Farmer Bob to gather enough rocks and branches to protect Furball's remains from hungry predators. Bear stepped forward, sniffed at her mother's body in the bundle of towels, and crouched, solemn and silent. After a few moments, she spoke.

"We will never again have such a capable leader as our alpha Furball. We release you to the other side, Mother, where Cinder waits to welcome you with open arms. May your skills, wisdom, deep love, and insight live on in me and future alphas. Goodbye, Mother," she whispered. Then she moved in front of the cat community, as its new alpha.

Farmer Bob and Leah's mimicked the cats' grief, their faces solemn and downcast.

"I'm so sorry this happened, Furball," Farmer Bob muttered. "You know that we love you!"

Leah took his hand and squeezed. "We will all miss you deeply, my Furball," she said, laying her other hand on the towel, "especially me."

The couple shoveled dirt over the cat's body and created a mound of rocks topped with tree branches. The humans remained after a few minutes of quiet. Being unable to get back in his truck, Farmer Bob worked some chores in the barn, and Leah return to feeding the cattle, working slower than usual, occasionally staring at the silent snow falling from the darkened sky.

The cats stayed behind, then headed back to the stone house, peeling off in quiet sorrow. Furball's family, as in a human funeral, stayed longer than the others.

The next spring, Leah planted catnip nearby which the cats enjoyed whenever they visited the community grave site. This site saw many funeral rituals, eventually for Puff, Bear, and many others. Eventually the tabby kitten would walk next to a new alpha, participating in the licking ceremony and offering comfort.

The feline community accepted death. Maybe, as Bear explained, it was because of their belief in the "Rainbow Bridge," their belief in a better existence.

Maybe it was their inherent knowledge of oneness with the physical universe, in which all living things are connected to all other parts of creation, even in death.

Regardless, despite their deep grief over the loss of their loved ones, the cats knew that life, one day, had to end for them, but that the community would survive with each new generation.

CHAPTER 7

Ivan

TRAGEDY IS NOT UNUSUAL when the toms, male cats, attempt to eliminate their competition by killing all the other toms' kittens. These outsider toms roam from farm to farm, looking to challenge all resident males in order to mate with their females. This natural instinct can threaten existing litters of kittens, whose mothers are usually helpless to intervene. Although something this awful would be unthinkable to humans, it's common among wild cats and even among Farmer Bob and Leah's farm cat community.

Sometimes, resident females handle these outside males on their own; sometimes, they are not able to. On one particular occasion while Furball was alpha, she and the other mothers worked together to try to thwart an outside male's attempt to take over. One morning, they made a horrible discovery: all the litters were sleeping in one of the bays in the barn, which had always been a safe place, when Cinnamon, one of Furball's many daughters, raced to those returning from their afternoon hunt.

"Our safe place has been invaded! The kittens are crying for their mothers, and worse, one of them is missing!"

"Sweet-ones," Furball questioned the litters, "who was here? Where is the littlest one?"

"We don't know!" the confused kittens wailed. "We were all sleeping when we heard lots of scuffling." Then one of the kittens was just gone. It happened so fast!"

Later that very week, another kidnapping occurred. This time, the kittens saw more. "A big, scary monster came and took him away," the kittens cried. "It was awful, Mama Furball."

All was quiet until a week later when the returning mothers heard the kittens' desperate cries yet again. This time there was more devastation, fur and wounded kittens littering the straw of the bay.

"The monster came back, and we saw him this time!" the kittens yelled. "He was big and hairy and so mean and so scary."

"I'm scared!" wailed one huddled in the shadowy corner. "We all are," chimed in the others.

As the mothers tried to calm them down, Furball called all the adult cats to a council meeting behind the stone house.

"Family, we are in a devastating crisis. This last attack is the third one in two weeks. One of my own babies was among the dead. " Furball focused on the ground in front of her, trying to calm her emotions before continuing. As alpha cat, she had to stay composed in every crisis. "We must put a stop to this carnage if the community is to survive." She hesitated for emphasis. "We don't want to scare the young ones. It could even be one of our own toms doing this. So we must move in secret."

Hunter, the lead short-haired cat, agreed, silently nodded her orange and black head. She had lost one of her own young in these attacks.

"I have a plan," Furball announced, "but I want to see what all of you think first."

"I say we find the murderer and kill him. No mercy!" yelled an immature voice from the back.

"I'll keep sentry and trade off. That way we can keep watch 24-7," suggested a tan and white female.

"I appreciate your suggestions," answered Furball, "but we should find out who is doing this before we make any other decisions. And we must do it in secret! We've been moving the litters every evening in order to fool this criminal, but the kittens are safe for only a little time because they make so much noise, so that is not a good solution."

Furball tensed her muscles, stood straighter, and pricked her feathered ears forward to alert the others of the next important part of her message.

"I suggest we put all new litters together in one nest and nurse them as needed. This will cause some confusion, but we have no choice. We must find a fortress for the litters that makes it difficult for marauding males to reach them, but we can get to the litters using hidden trails only the mothers know about."

"That's a great idea!" Cinnamon agreed. "We could create an obstacle course of sorts, to make it harder to get to the little ones."

"Just yesterday, I saw Farmer Bob place a cattle trailer next to the hay stalls," offered Yellow Cat. "That might be perfect! It's roomy with lots of hay to hide and burrow in. Also, it has steep walls, so it's not easy to get in or out of. It'll be hard to get the kittens in, but if you jump up on the tires first, I think all of you will be able to carry your kittens through the slits at the top of the walls." Furball smiled. Gentle Yellow Kitty was her favorite friend.

That evening, after the mothers had a chance to inspect the rusty cattle trailer, they unanimously agreed it was the ideal fortress and steep walls with separated boards for a roof the guardians could look down into. Soon, all the litters were safely snuggled in with plenty of hay for camouflage.

Later that week, Furball discovered a suspicious odor of urine used to mark territory on the trailer. She couldn't identify the source but warned the others to be particularly alert to any hint of a stranger nearby. She assigned Yellow Kitty to watch and warn the others if someone suspicious was lurking near the new home.

It happened the very next day. On patrol, Yellow Kitty had just lain down in the speckled sunlight filtering through leaves of surrounding oak trees when directly behind him, he heard what sounded like the wind moving the leaves on the ground followed by muffled padding on the wheel covering. Then he heard scratching sounds as something made its way up the side of the outer wall. It reached the top and was immediately inside landing with an "umph" on the floor.

Without hesitating, Yellow Kitty screamed his warning. "Yeaow! Yeaow! Come quick! Hurry! Trespasser!" He heard the mews of the kittens, who must have thought the animal was a mother cat. As he catapulted himself to the top, the mothers collected at the foot of the trailer, Furball in the lead.

They screamed and yowled as they reached the top and peered down into the trailer. The tom was tawny brown with lean sides and a streak of white running down his face to his lips, where he carried one of the tiniest kittens. He turned around, surprised at all the cats dropping into the trailer. As if in a precise ballet, they circled him, moving counter clockwise, snarling and hissing, as they waited for Furball's order to attack.

The tom saw angry mothers everywhere he looked. Carefully, keeping his eyes on them in their almost step-for-step movement, he let the baby drop soundlessly from his mouth. It wiggled clumsily back to the nest, where the others scooted far into the corner under the hay to hide.

With the scared kitten safely back in the nest, Furball cried, "Ladies, it's pay-back time!" and they attacked. Scratching, hissing, and tearing into the tom, the mothers fought until, within just seconds, he lay helpless, gasping for breath.

"Let's kill the murderer!" cried one of the mothers who'd lost a kitten the previous week.

"Wait. I think he's learned not to mess with us farm cats," Furball said. "Get him out of here!" she called to the male cats waiting outside.

"Well, mothers, you certainly took care of that tom!"

announced Yellow Kitty with admiration as he and the other males started to drag the tom out of the trailer. Like most of the other resident males, Yellow Kitty had never threatened any of the other members. These farm community males had a deep respect for Furball. They would challenge each other, sending some of the losers off the farm, but they never bothered the ladies. "Lovers, not fighters," they called themselves. With their cooperative impulses, bravery, and strong alpha leadership, the farm cat community survived many such attacks. But they didn't always win. Sometimes, even when they did their best, the community failed.

One such failure involved an ebony tom whose behavior was more than natural instinct. This tom's reign of terror was much more malicious than an attempted takeover: it was deliberately evil.

Ivan's arrival at the farm lives in their history to this day. If a mother or father needs to instill fear in a kitten or adolescent, they warn, "Do that again and Ivan the Terrible will come and get you tonight." To all the cats, he proves the very existence of incarnate evil.

This raven-colored, handsome cat appeared several generations after Furball's reign. Some considered her absence the reason that running Ivan off proved impossible. Some thought he emerged from another realm, diabolical and unearthly. Others just shook their heads in sadness at the very mention of his name.

The day he arrived was like any other. Birds were eagerly singing, and the late winter sun was just starting to warm the hard earth and melt the drifts of snow, rivulets of snowmelt and mud creating deep crevices down the bumpy driveway.

"Hey, look at the new tom," said Leah to Farmer Bob when the black cat jumped up on the porch stoop.

"Yeah, look at his beautiful raven-colored fur. He's a handsome specimen, isn't he?"

"And he's such a friendly boy!" Leah commented as she bent down to stroke him as he rubbed his body and curled his tail affectionately around her legs. He looked up at her with soft eyes. "Mew? Mew?" he asked hungrily, wandering over to the group of cats and waiting patiently for them to get their fill from the dinner plate before he ate. "He's a courteous guy," observed Farmer Bob. "He'll be quite a good pick to father the next generation. But I wonder—"

"Let's hope he doesn't threaten the other males too much. He looks strong as well as handsome."

Later that evening, storm clouds hid the sun, and the wind picked up significantly. Most of the other cats were enjoying the last of the day's waning sunlight, resting their eyes or grooming themselves with full bellies. The new tom sat motionless, attentively watching Leah and Farmer Bob rumbling down the driveway and out on the main road while he surveyed the others in the yard in front of the stone house. His steely, almost glowing, eyes finally narrowed on one of the smaller, resident males: a longhaired cat who had just reached maturity named Gray for his blue-gray coat. Gray was lazing in the yard, his eyes almost closed in contentment, unaware of the unblinking stare of the newcomer.

The black tom transformed from the passive, friendly fellow the humans had just encountered. His eyes had changed from wide-eyed innocence to narrowed slits and pinpricks pupils. A smirk formed at the corners of his mouth. His tall, stone-like posture deliberately projected egotistical self-assurance. Then, for no reason in particular, the tom marched deliberately but unhurried to Gray.

"Hey, you! Puny excuse for a tom!" he growled menacingly, making himself a huge, looming presence. "I'm the main male here now," he snarled.

In a submissive position, Gray lay with his legs up to protect himself. Without waiting for a reply, the black tom snapped down with his teeth on one of Gray's hind legs and shook him violently until a loud cracking sound echoed through the barnyard. The wounded cat screamed in pain and fled with his leg dangling behind him.

"Serves him right!" snorted the attacker with a satisfied grimace. "He was the ugliest cat I've ever seen! Any other ugly cats around here?" he challenged loudly. All the other cats melted into the shadows.

Things quieted as the newcomer waited for things to calm down. But it wasn't long before the pattern continued. By day, he socialized with soft purrs and gentle rubs against the humans, but when they left for the day, he morphed into a black devil.

He strode through the yard, seeking out the weakest or smallest to eliminate, efficient as an invading army. He didn't fight fairly, using surprise and intimidation to his advantage.

One time, he chased another male into a corner of a bay, eyed him with his famous red-eyed stare, and stepped very slowly but unwaveringly toward the cowering cat, trying to make himself as small as possible.

"What's the matter? Can't you do anything but cringe in the corner?" he hissed. Even though the cornered cat quickly raised his paws with claws and growled in return with flat ears, the sable cat struck in a flash, grabbing his front leg just above the paw and biting so hard his leg cracked almost in half. When the cat tried to flee, he continued to tear whatever he could until the other was able to escape with a broken paw and multiple bloody wounds. As the black tom twirled around and stalked off, he muttered, "I hate cowards! I hate the weak!"

After two weeks of these violent rages, he could mate with any female of his choosing. The other toms dared not challenge him. Sometimes, he was unnecessarily brutal with the females as well, leaving open wounds that often became infected. Leah and Farmer Bob had never seen such injuries but couldn't figure out what was causing them. They couldn't believe that it was the new tom. He always made sure he fooled the humans with innocent purring and affectionate rubbing. But when they were gone, he went back to his evil work.

Things finally came to a head when he challenged a yellow tabby called "Fred the Cat." Fred, a gentle giant, always allowed the females to eat first and asked for their permission to mate with them with a soft rub on their heads. One female was sure she'd heard him say, "Thank you," after a coupling when he licked her head with tender care—something toms never did.

Fred also refused to fight it out with competing males, preferring to gently woo the females with his tender offers of love. Fred even hung out in the window well with the females and some of the kittens in order to defend them from the black cat's wild rages.

So it was no surprise that Fred the Cat suffered more than all the others from the sable tom's brutality. By the end of the attack, Fred was left for dead, flaps of fur hanging from bloody wounds and a badly injured back leg. Leah found him in the window well when she arrived the next morning. Angry at the sight of his ruined body, she took him into the stone house, nursed his wounds with antiseptic lotion after a visit to the vet, and gave him shots of antibiotics. This care went on for months.

Once, when Fred the Cat was allowed out to sunbathe on the stone house step, Dianna, the reigning alpha, asked him if the humans should "make the black one go away." Unbelievably, the gentle tiger urged tolerance for "that crazy cat!"

Leah spent many afternoons washing and cleaning the deeply infected injuries. Despite her efforts, Fred the Cat died like many of the other cats the tom had butchered. After his death, Leah was inconsolable with grief and anger. By now, she and Farmer Bob suspected that the black tom was deceiving: maiming cats after flattering them with sweet meows and curls of his tail around their legs.

Only once did the black one face any kind of direct challenge from a farm cat. By the time the community had dwindled down to a few females, Dianna finally faced him.

"You must stop this evil!" she raged. "You don't just challenge and fight fairly; you maim and deliberately inflict horrible pain. In fact, I don't think you want to kill as much as disable and make others suffer! You are pure evil!"

The grimacing tom seemed amused at her words. He puffed out his sleek chest and curled his upper lip.

"I eliminate all rivals! I have no concern for their pain! I make sure it is the worst they have ever experienced—if I allow them to live!" His defiant scowl seemed like a stone face. "What exactly are you going to do about it?" he asked.

The alpha steadily backed away until the tom lost patience and pushed past her, stomping proudly toward the stone house. Staring after him, she hissed, but it was no use. "There is no stopping this malicious cat!"

Eventually, the tom had grown so arrogant that he started fights before Leah and Farmer Bob were out of sight.

"That tom is a black devil," Leah said to Farmer Bob. "He's been responsible for how many killings? And if he doesn't kill them, he cripples them for life. Like our poor old Gray. And look what he did to Fred the Cat! He's even brutal with the girls. That monster should be called 'Ivan the Terrible.'"

Farmer Bob nodded in agreement. "Sandi called from the next farm. Apparently Ivan attacked some of her cats too. In fact, they are losing cats just like we are! This can't go on!"

"If he were human, he'd have no conscience. Certainly no mercy. As if he enjoys the suffering he causes. And then he acts all friendly and cute with us. What a monster! What are we going to do? Can we do anything?" Leah moaned.

"I've never seen such a cruel animal of any species, and I've been farming a long time. But don't worry, Leah. He always rubs against my leg, so that will make him easy to catch. He won't be working his wickedness anymore when I'm done with him."

Later that evening, the cats watched with curiosity when Farmer Bob petted Ivan and talked gently to him. When Ivan circled his legs, purring loudly, Farmer Bob snatched him up! Ivan squirmed to get loose. He knew something wasn't right, but there was no escaping. Farmer Bob grimly grabbed his gun, took the struggling cat into the truck's cab, and backed down the driveway and disappeared. Not long after, Farmer Bob returned. Without Ivan. And no one ever saw Ivan the Terrible again.

In his wake, Ivan left a terrified community with a helpless alpha and, worst of all, some very aggressive, dark-colored kittens. It took many, many generations until all the meanness was bred out of the cats, so peace eventually returned to the farm. Stories of Ivan grew to mythic proportions. No one ever forgot "Ivan the Terrible," the essence of evil.

Ivan

CHAPTER 8

FDR

OUR HERO WAS BORN JUST ANOTHER ORDINARY FARM CAT. He descended from Hunter's family, but unlike his aunt Dianna, he had no aspirations to be an alpha. He'd leave that honor to the long-haired family.

He was mousey gray with white tips on his nose and paws as if he'd curiously explored some spilt white paint. He could hunt with some degree of success but didn't have unusual athletic skills like Hunter, his grandmother; Blue Eyes, his mother; or Dianna. He had no exceptional markings, abilities, or traits that distinguished him, so no one thought there was anything extraordinary about him.

However, he could claim at least one unusual fact: his sister, Blind Kitty, was almost totally blind. She resembled her brother in that her fur was a mottled gray with muted spots of faded orange and off-white. No one knew if she'd been born blind or just developed weak, weepy eyes common in some farm cats. It may be that she had some faint vision for movement or blurred images, but her moist eyes were always only slits. And although she couldn't see, she could maneuver around the farm with ease. So, for the most part, the other fully-functioning cats ignored her.

Naturally, Blind Kitty gravitated to her brother, sticking close to him, for protection and companionship. When others crowded her out of the dinner dish, her brother would shift slightly to one side, giving her enough room to eat. He also shared his kills from the hunt with her, leaving the meatiest parts near her nose, so she could smell and devour it. He always found time to play with her tail or rough-house with her, the two twisting and turning in a tight knot just like normal siblings. But if she objected with a sharp "Meow" or couldn't get away from him, he'd always immediately back off and lick her ears in apology.

He was also vigilant to prevent any teasing and bullying. If another cat tried to snatch food away from her or become rough with her, he would step between them, hair raised along his spine, managing to look large and formidable. He'd glare directly into the other's eyes, remaining rigid until it backed off. Afterwards, he would groom his sister, especially around her eyes, licking away the discharge that accumulated there. At night, they always slept tightly woven together, just like kittens. Except when hunting, he was always found near his sister.

One late afternoon, as all the cats trailed in from hunting, he was not among them.

"Has anyone seen my brother?" Blind Kitty cried desperately. "He must not have come back because he always checks in with me after the hunt. And he hasn't today. Has anyone seen him?"

The returning cats just stepped around her, completely ignoring her pleas. Later, there was no one to help her find space around the dinner dish, so she was nudged aside. She went hungry that night. There was no one to groom her after dinner either, so she had to wipe her own eyes with her moistened front paws. There wasn't anyone to snuggle with in the musty hay either. She'd never been so lonely in all her life!

The next day, Leah saw her hanging around the stone house by herself, squinting in the direction of the wide fields beyond the ravine where the cats had last hunted.

"What's the matter, Blind Kitty?" she asked. "I know your

brother didn't return yesterday. Are you worried about him?" Leah bent down, offering the blind cat a comforting scratch under her chin. "Don't worry! He would never leave you by yourself. He'll show up!"

And he did. But something was very wrong. That afternoon, he emerged from the ravine, crawling, pulling himself forward by his front feet, his hind legs dragging helplessly behind him on the ground like a rag doll.

"Oh, no! What's happened?" cried Leah when she saw him.

"What's wrong?" cried his sister, sniffing at his torso and limp back legs.

His hind legs were twitching constantly as if some impulse was trying to bring his legs back to life. One leg lay across the other in a cross like stacked wood. "Nothing I can't handle, Sis. Just a little accident," he responded casually. "I'm not sure what exactly happened. I think I got too close to one of the cattle, and it stepped on my back. After that I couldn't feel my legs. But there's no pain, Sis. It just took such a long time to get home because I had to rest. A lot!"

"Are you going to be okay?" Blind Kitty wanted to know. She could tell from sound of his voice that he was prone, but his image was a blur.

"Oh, I'll be fine. My hunting days are over though. But I can still maneuver around the farm using my front legs! We'll be fine, Sis. Come here and stick close to me, just like usual."

Thin Blind Kitty found her way to his side and nuzzled him along his body until she got to his legs. She sniffed each one carefully.

"They're twitching but not moving like they should." She licked each leg, pausing to sense their positions. Then she sat back on her haunches.

"How are we going to eat? How are we going to survive if both of us can't take care of ourselves?" she moaned.

"Sis, I have friends who will bring us some food from the hunt. In fact, I've never told you this, but even when I was healthy and wasn't able to get a meal for you, they shared their own kill with me. Plus, Leah always feeds us and keeps close watch over us cats. You know that." He leaned up to his sister's face and reassuringly licked her lower chin. "See! I can still groom. We'll be fine!"

As he promised, he carried on as if he were his usual healthy self. At dinner, he was able to nudge the more assertive cats away with surprising strength, easily eating from his lowered height while the other cats obliged them by moving aside for Blind Kitty to squeeze in for her share. The two still play-tussled together, chewing each other's neck and grabbing each other's body, but now Blind Kitty was the one careful not to hurt her sibling, backing off when he couldn't get a grip on her or seemed frustrated. He even managed to play-fight with his peers, often on his back with his legs raised in the air, scuffling with them just as he has done before.

He groomed his upper body and his sister's face when she placed herself near enough, but now Blind Kitty made sure to reciprocate by licking his face and lower body until he was clean. She chose where to sleep in the warm hay, making the bedding low, so he could pull himself into their sleeping area. Then, when he got settled, she would wrap herself around him and lay her head on his lower body. The constant twitching of his legs never bothered her.

Although his sister would never admit it, their roles were reversed. It was she who accommodated him now. It was Blind Kitty who protected them from bullying or disrespectful cats, calling to the others to stop and talk with him and growl if they didn't give him room at the dinner dish.

"I might not be able to see, but I know what's going on," she said one day to a group of toms. "You guys need to pay attention and be nice to my brother—just like before! His life isn't easy now. I know he tries to act like he did before, like nothing's changed, but we know differently. We have to be kind to him and to help him when he's hungry or needs grooming."

"Yeah, yeah," the others murmured dismissively.

At first, nothing changed; they didn't pay any more attention to him or Blind Kitty than before.

But after a while, they gradually became more attentive to him. For instance, one of his best friends, a black-and-white tuxedo cat, started telling him the latest farm news, like the cattle escaping and wandering onto the road while Farmer Bob ran after them trying to corral them. The two laughed heartily at the sight!

Over time, this kind of acceptance and comradeship encouraged the others to talk with the wounded cat too. Soon he and his friends were laughing about the latest clumsy sparring between the adolescent males or their escapades with neighboring females or scuffles with a nosy neighbor cat.

It seemed he had regained his previous status despite his injury. The other cats stopped to discuss their business with him, leaning close to the ground in order to communicate. After the hunt, they shared stories of their near-misses with our hero in the middle of their circle. And always after the sharing, prime bits of the kill were left behind. Most importantly, they never mocked him or left him out of their activities. Not only did they show him respect; they showed him admiration as well.

But with time, the wounded cat shrunk from his previous bulk. Not only was he getting little exercise; he wasn't eating nearly as much either. Now his sister was noticeably larger.

"Are you okay?" she asked one day. "You sometimes seem discouraged or maybe even sad. I'm really worried about you!" Then she softly nuzzled his skinny neck and licked his ears.

Her brother sighed.

"I admit that, sometimes just moving is hard work! I have to pull myself everywhere. But that just means I need to rest at times. It must look as if I am disheartened, but I'm not really; I just have to keep working and moving to try and keep up. I know you can't see me clearly, but I can do most of what is necessary to survive. With yours and Leah's help! I'm just tired," he reassured her. "Besides, Sis, if you can manage to take care of us both, I'm sure that I'll be thriving again someday soon!" He smiled and returned her affection, licking her face.

One particular cat became an especially close friend of the paralyzed cat. Before the accident, our hero didn't even notice this cat, who never mattered in his cadre of friends. This cat couldn't walk well either; he'd been maimed by Ivan during his reign of terror. Crippled by Ivan's fierce bite, he was left with a paw that permanently hung limp from his upper foreleg. But he'd figured out how to get around the farm pretty quickly by lightly touching the bad paw to the ground for balance, but not for putting any weight on it. He could hobble pretty well to the food bowl and to his favorite spot in the sun. And Leah still loved him, renaming him "Crippled Kitty."

Crippled Kitty paid close attention to his paralyzed friend, helping him get enough food by pushing some of the other hungry cats aside and even helping Blind Kitty keep him clean in the hard-to-reach places. When our hero managed to pull himself up to the stone house step, Crippled Kitty would often lie somewhere on the step too. He always placed himself near enough to him if he needed help. So between Blind Kitty, Crippled Kitty, and his other friends, our hero was almost never alone and was always well taken care of.

Leah also kept her eye on the paralyzed cat. Whenever she brought out some delicious chicken treats, she made sure that they ate first, leaning over and talking gently to the group, asking how their day was.

The entire cat community, even the kittens, followed his caregivers' example, making way for the trio at the food bowl, bringing home some of their kill, and even grooming them with their gentle tongues, and always taking care not to step on or push them. One of the black-and-white tuxedo kittens loved to chase their moving tails, usually ending the game laying closely tucked into a furry side. It spent hours listening to the prone cat tell stories of him and his sister's growing up together, the fun of hunting for rabbits, and meeting the daily challenges of participating in the cat community. Enthralled with his adventures, the kitten listened with rapt attention, never interrupting his favorite adult.

Even though these three received special attention, they never took advantage of their special treatment. Instead, they handled themselves like the other healthy cats. Our hero would grab food from the others just like they did with each other, and he wouldn't let any of them take Leah's treats of cheese away from Crippled Kitty or his sister if they unintentionally got too pushy.

"Hey, guys! Back off!" he'd yowl. "We have two mouths to feed here. Wait your turn!" Being admonished, the others would draw back respectfully.

Late one evening, after the chores had been completed, Leah and Farmer Bob sat in the rusted, metal chairs in front of the stone house watching the cats rest after their evening meal. The three were grooming each other in the waning sun.

"The paralyzed cat tries so hard to act like the other normal cats. He pulls himself everywhere, tussles with his buddies, and cares for his sister and Crippled Kitty in any way he can, like when he lays on the food dish, so the other two can eat first. He's determined to do just about anything to prove he can take care of himself. And the others too," pointed out Farmer Bob.

"You know, he reminds me of Franklin D. Roosevelt."

Remember? That man carried huge responsibilities as president even though he was crippled by polio. He insisted on being propped up in his leg braces when giving a speech, so he'd appear to be standing on his own. Such endurance during our country's trying times—he was amazing!" Leah paused, grinning at the trio lazing in the fading sun. "Let's call him FDR. Just like the real FDR: determined, no self-pity despite his difficult life. Maybe Blind Kitty and Crippled Kitty could be his Cabinet?" Leah laughed at the thought.

So FDR, Blind Kitty, and Crippled Kitty lived in their own group but still interacted with the cat community as if they were perfectly healthy. The community treated them with respect, deference and even admiration. Similar to his name sake, FDR was indeed an ordinary cat; he survived despite his injury. FDR lived an extraordinary life.

FDR

CHAPTER 9

Ghost Eyes

AS GENERATIONS WERE BORN, LIVED, AND DIED, the farm's cat community changed in composition and character, depending on the personality of the alpha and significant events, such as the disastrous changes affected by Ivan's reign of terror. The only constants were Leah and Farmer Bob. The original characteristics of the long-haired family could not be preserved, so the family weakened with each generation until their long, silky fur; luxurious whiskers; and chattiness became too difficult to identify, leading to apparent extinction.

Gradually, as different males visited the farm and different alphas ruled, a number of different colors and shapes—Siamese, black as a starless night, and black-and-white tuxedo cats, among many other variations—replaced this family. The scene at the evening food bowl vibrated a living, vivid patchwork quilt. The lineage originating from the huge, long-haired Stranger and Cinder all but disappeared as Furball, Bear, and successive long-haired alphas died out.

All farm cat communities suffer disasters from natural causes such as marauding males wanting to insure their own line of kittens or brutal attacks by predators that can destroy an entire cat community. This darkest tragedy occurred one night on the farm cat community, leaving not a single member of the short or long-haired clans alive. Leah, after finding all her cats dead, wept uncontrollably, vowing never to care for a cat community ever again.

A week later, just as Leah was emerging from her grief, she heard faint but discernible mews coming from the back of the rickety, rusted wagon Farmer Bob used to haul feed and other heavy materials.

Leah approached the sound, curiosity etched across her face, hope surfacing in her eyes. Bending down, she peered into the wagon's open end. Out of the layers of moldy leaves and tattered scraps of burlap popped a surviving female with a tiny spot of black in her mouth, and her kitten mewing, urgently.

"Oh my, you two did survive!" Leah giggled with delight.

She scooped up the kitten that was deposited at her feet. It scrambled and scratched to escape, but she held it closely to her chest as she soothed the mother by rubbing her chin. "So, brave mama, you escaped with your little one. You rescued it from that brutality; you must have run fast and hard. And look at this little Bad Boy! He is one scrappy cat. I imagine he'll fight just about anything after that experience."

The mother cried nervously for the return of her kitten, so Leah slowly set the complaining kitten on the wagon's floorboards, allowing its overprotective mother to inspect and reclaim it.

Within just a few months, the cat community started to regenerate and grew exponentially, but it never recovered the clearly discernible long-haired traits until,—

"I appeared, that is" explained Ghost Eyes, "within a generation or two of the disaster. I didn't really think of myself as a long-hair until one day, when Leah closely inspected me. 'Look at those mysterious eyes and all that hair!' she exclaimed.

"Then, one evening, as the sun dipped behind the tree line, I lingered after a community meal and rubbed against Leah's multicolored boots. I stared at her, eye to eye. When she recognized my plea to be held, she scooped me up like a pile of dried leaves and hugged me to her chest. I rubbed my cheek against hers, mewing my gratitude for the evening's meal.

"You remind me so much of your ancestor, Furball," she said. "She used to do the same thing." Then she looked closer. "You know, your limbs are not very heavy, but the solid bone structure of the long-hairs is there. And those never-ending whiskers and ears decorated with delicate, sideways hair. And that incessant chattering...so typical of the family. What music to my ears!" I took all this information in as I snuggled into her tightly folded arms. There was no doubting my proud heritage.

"One day, as I crossed the creek, I looked into its still, transparent water hoping to snag an unsuspecting minnow. I was startled by my unusual eyes peeking out from the furred shelf of my eyelids. Those shadowy, half-mast eyes reflected a gloomy look, one of deep and prolonged sadness. Or perhaps an uncanny seriousness. I'm not sure which or why. Maybe it was grief for the lost generations? Maybe because I'm alone? Soon afterwards, Leah named me 'Ghost Eyes.'

"I don't have any of the usual feline drama in my life, like so many on the farm. Instead, I keep things simple. I hunt and fight and follow Leah around and then disappear into the day, visiting my favorite gals at Ashley's house and beyond. But all it takes is to hear Leah's distant call, 'Here, kitties! Come, Ghost Eyes! Come!' for me to lope through the tall weeds of the field, leap over the creek, and head up the hill from the ravine to her, 'chattering' my excitement for dinner. Often Leah and I go into the stone house, so I can eat away from the other cats, in peace and settle down for a nice talk with Leah on the stone house's steps, my eyelids drooping with contentment.

"I also avoid conflict as much as I can, unlike most other cats. No brushes with death. No wandering back to the farm after disappearing for weeks. No guarding against prey from the sky or run-ins with predators bent on destroying the community. No alpha responsibilities. And certainly no visits to a distant city.

"However, as the lone remaining ancestor, I have a serious responsibility: I must now assure my family's survival. Leah says my ghost eyes open a window into the past of the long-hair clan that have come and gone, enduring specters of heartbreak and triumphs of survival.

"But, mostly, my eyes visualize a future for Farmer Bob and Leah's cat community. When I too cross the 'Rainbow Bridge,' I know there will be my offspring to carry on the long-hairs' traditions.

"In fact, just the other day on the farm, I saw a handsome black-and-white young tom with sweeping white whiskers radiating from its eyes and mouth like spikes on a weed. His striking beauty and confident marching, instead of just walking, harked back to the long-haired clan along with his tufted ears, white paws and a nose spattered with black spots. When he stopped his searching of the yard for a sibling to tussle with, his proud eyes stared at me with some sort of distant recognition. I smiled to myself as I actually saw the image of that famous long-haired Stranger. Then the tom saw Leah with the rubber dish and bounced after her, complaining loudly at her slowness. Our Leah bent over the scolding cat, smiled affectionately and called, 'Come, kitties! Everyone come! Come!'"

Ghost Eyes

Made in the USA
Lexington, KY
09 August 2018